Short Story International

Tales by the World's Great Contemporary Writers Presented Unabridged

All selections in
Short Story International
are reprinted full and
unabridged in the author's
own words. Nothing is
added, subtracted,
condensed or rewritten.

Volume 6, Number 35, December 1982
Short Story International (USPS 375-970)

Second-class postage paid at Great Neck, N.Y. 11022 and at additional mailing offices. **Editorial offices: P.O. Box 405, Great Neck, N.Y. 11022.** Enclose stamped, self-addressed envelope with previously published stories submitted for possible reprinting in *Short Story International*. Please note *SSI* does not accept unpublished original manuscripts. One year (six issues) subscription for U.S., U.S. possessions $16, Canada $18 (US), other countries $21 (US). All institutions add $2 per annual subscription. Single copy price $3.45. **For subscriptions and address changes write to *Short Story International*. P.O. Box 405, Great Neck, N.Y. 11022.** *Short Story International* is published bimonthly by International Cultural Exchange, 6 Sheffield Road, Great Neck, N.Y. 11021. Postmaster please send Form 3579 to P.O. Box 405, Great Neck, N.Y. 11022.

Note from the Editor

For some months we had been searching for a more straightforward cover design for *Short Story International.* The flow of incoming subscribers' mail and a chunk of research clinched the change reflected in this issue. We are confident the simplicity and dignity of our new face will find favor.

With the cover restyled, our attention is focusing on the upcoming holiday and gift shopping season. Recalling stories of frenzy, fatigue and agitation last year, we direct your attention to pages 165 and 167 of this issue.

Gift subscriptions of *SSI* and its two younger-reader editions, *Seedling Series* and *Student Series,* may be the answer to that gnawing problem of an appropriate gift. Of course, cards announcing your gift are sent.

The arrival of each issue—throughout the year—will be a reminder of your thoughtfulness.

Copyrights and acknowledgments

We wish to express deep thanks to the authors, publishers, translators and literary agents for their permission to reprint the stories in this issue.

"Strangers' Country" from *Strangers' Country and Other Stories* by Geoffrey Dean. Copyright Geoffrey Dean. Reprinted by permission. "The Granny Room" by John Haylock first appeared in *Blackwood's Magazine.* Copyright 1980 John Haylock. Reprinted by permission of the author and editor of *Blackwood's Magazine.* "Dear Truth" by Ali Shalash. Translation by Ali Shalash 1982. "The Tide Woman" by Frøydis Petersen, translation by Dorrit Berg, first appeared in *Scandinavian Review,* No. 2, 1981. Reprinted by permission of the American-Scandinavian Foundation. "Waywaya" from *Waywaya and Other Stories from the Philippines* by F. Sionil José. Copyright © F. Sionil José 1980. Reprinted by permission of Heinemann Educational Books (Asia) Ltd. "Inglés" from *Nie strzelaj do organisty* by Maria Nurowska. English translation by Edward Rothert first appeared in *Polish Perspectives,* 1976. Copyright Maria Nurowska. Reprinted by permission of the author and Authors' Agency Ltd. "Give and Take" by Paul Dobson first appeared in *Fair Lady.* Copyright © 1979 Paul Dobson. "The Arrival of Autumn in Constantinople" by Norberto Luis Romero. English translation by H.E. Francis first appeared in *Mississippi Review,* 1980. Reprinted by permission. "The Operation" by Pensri Kiengsiri from *Taw and Other Thai Stories,* ed. Jennifer Draskau. Translation © H.E.B. 1975. Reprinted by permission of Heinemann Educational Books (Asia) Ltd. "The Grand Illumination" from *Cast of Characters* by Garson Kanin. Copyright © 1969 T.F.T. Corporation. Published by Atheneum. "All the Way" by Penelope Garlick © 1982 Penelope Garlick.

Photo credits: John Haylock by Ian Buruma.

Table of Contents

“Perhaps that was the time when it all began.”

Strangers’ Country

BY GEOFFREY DEAN

HE was blown in perhaps, by the night’s storm. Deposited there, on the Post Office steps and when the darkness retreated and the new morning sun steamed the streets, he became visible to the people of the town.

His pin-striped suit, three buttoned up, gleamed and winked with a translucent thread, and underneath, his black shirt added more darkness to his face.

“Who’s the dago?”

“How’d I know?”

They booted their way past, footpaths ringing, voices fading.

“Cop the shoes!”

“How’d y’like to get stowed with one of them on a frosty morning?”

Helmets and lamps swinging jauntily from their belts, they disappeared towards the hills, the mines, the blackest caves of the earth.

They called him Iti' to his face, the dago behind his back, and those more tolerant, or seemingly so, called him "The Italian." They found him a job on the hoppers, pulling levers that shot tons of coal into the iron trucks.

The dust rose in great choking clouds. It settled on his clothing, and on every exposed part of his skin.

"Strewth, y'couldn't find him on a dark night," a shift boss said. "He could be in bed with me missus and I'd never know."

He was accepted nevertheless, not as a friend, but neither as a stranger. He was simply there, existing in his dumb solitude like a stray but familiar dog.

"The Italian will load her."

"I saw Iti' havin' a beer th'other night—didn't seem to go on'er much—misses his vino I reckon."

The Italian went to the pictures. He sat quiet and aloof in the far back corner. Sometimes afraid under the staring white lights, always bewildered, as if he was lost and too shy to ask the way. He couldn't have asked the way anyway—he couldn't speak English. Yet he sat and watched the players on the screen with obvious enjoyment, his blue-black shiny jaws working incessantly on a mouth full of chewing gum. He stood for the Queen, reverent, erect and ramrod; then he was gone, quick as a blink up the road to the pub, to be swallowed for another week by his lonely foreign room.

But the dust got into his lungs, he choked on it and vomited up black bile at nights. He coughed in the lavatories. He coughed in his cold sullen room. The lonely night-still sound of his coughing echoed along the empty halls...

"Why don't he go to the quack?"

He would not have known the way, or what to say...

"I'll take him me-self. S'help me—it's drivin' me MacRobinson. I'll take him t'morrow."

It was found that his lungs were weak, and the coal dust could kill him. It was also found that he had spent his childhood on a farm in Southern Italy. A committee in the town financed him to an old motorbike and sidecar, and by degrees they integrated him into the farming community. Each morning at sunrise the main street was hammered by the sounds of the ancient bike taking off to a distant farm. And those who bothered could have looked out and seen the Italian crouched over the thundering machine like an excited monkey, his eyes fixed resolutely ahead to the country roads and the rising blue hills...

"I've hired the Italian for a few months, live in," Albert said.

Doris looked at her husband with disbelief.

"To do the fences. Why not, they say he's pretty good?"

"You'll get some fancy fencing now," Doris said. "And what am I going to feed him on, spaghetti?"

"Thought I'd start killing that small mob of ewes." His voice sounded peevish.

Doris went back to the kitchen to grumble amongst her pots and pans. She tried to remember all she could about Italy—a geography lesson somewhere in the school-dim past.

But they had faded, those facts and figures that accounted for education. Now it was nothing but the memory, smells of dust and sleepy warmth of sun through multiple windows. Education was the fading, droning voice, lost in the half-light of youth.

As the boys she had known in Ginney's Gully were lost. The trembling boys, with downcast eyes who had fumbled with her dress and smudged her pants, then stopped trembling and no longer cared. It was never like it was supposed to be and the boys were not to blame. Cowboys and Indians last week, men and lovers this week; they should have kept their toy guns on for a few more years, hunted rabbits with catapults, home-made bows and arrows; anything to keep their flies buttoned-up, and their eyes only for the white tails of rabbits skidding through the tussock grass.

They had forgotten her, and Doris had returned to the tear-stained pages of "True Love." But fictional love had been as unsatisfactory as the trembling boys; soon forgotten, the box of books had burned with the other leftovers in the incinerator at the bottom of the garden. Doris, cast up by life at an early age retreated into a serenity of neck-buttoned dresses, hidden knees, and sermon-filled Sundays. She was finally married, high-necked, in tulle and lace; white and unblushingly virginal to a husband who wouldn't know either way. There was a honeymoon in a boarding house by the sea and Doris found her only romance on the third day, in a piece of music. She heard the notes, pure and transparent as light, falling in the room and fading across the sea at sunset.

There on the bed with her husband who was now silent, undemanding, forgotten. She lay and listened, seeing from the window the sun strike red and orange on the castle of cliffs and for a few short minutes a mystery was revealed to her, out there, in the darkening sea...

The sound of a motorbike chugging into the yard brought her thoughts back with a shock. She saw the dusty machine as it passed the window. Her hands hovered above the dishes, indecisive. Should she go out with Alfred and make the stranger welcome? She decided not to, and for the moment was content to catch a glimpse of him through the perforated curtains across the window.

"Well, if he ain't a little bloke," she thought, overcoming a strong desire to push the window open and get a better look.

"Soon enough," she said aloud, and went out into the sunroom to feed her baby. She sat in the sun with the babe at her breast and thought plesantly, and quite inaccurately, of distant Italy.

That morning Doris took extra pains to shine and dust, and when she thought about it, she smiled to herself. "Doris you're putting on a show for a little foreign beggar who looks like a monkey."

It was all pretty silly.

But when she cooked the dinner she put in a few little extras, like thyme in the roast and a little powdered rosemary (where it came from she couldn't remember); she even poured a little sherry over the custard because she suspected Italians liked it that way.

They came in at twelve-thirty; her husband stamping his boots half-heartedly on the doormat and trampling most of the mud into the kitchen and the Italian following, wiping his boots delicately, rubbing first the soles, then along each side. He looked uncomfortable in the thick boots, as if their size and weight worried him.

"Wash in the laundry," Albert said loudly. He rolled his sleeves back and went through the motions of scrubbing. The Italian nodded and smiled. He smiled at the room, at Doris, at the baby in the pram.

He went on smiling all the way to the laundry.

Doris shook her head in wonder and began setting the table. Once she caught a glimpse of the Italian, he was shirtless, and the water dripped from arms and shoulders that were smooth-brown and dully gleaming, like polished wood.

"Gawd," Doris thought, looking down at her own white lightly freckled arms. "He's almost black."

They sat at the table. Doris the essence of a good hostess, plied the stranger with food and smiled at him, like one would encourage a shy child. He ate delicately, cutting his meat into small pieces and transferring them to his mouth one at a time. He held his knife and fork in a strange manner, grasping them with a full hand yet gently, as one holds a pen.

"I suppose he's used to chopsticks," Doris thought. "Or was that China?"

Albert signified his meal finished by dropping his knife and fork with a clatter and pushing his plate away.

"That was good," he said. He smacked his lips and laughed. He turned to the Italian. "Good tucker, eh Iti'?"

The Italian hearing one word familiar to him, looked up and smiled, half-enquiring, half-embarrassed. His teeth white and even, shone for a moment then disappeared.

"Like a pup," thought Doris, "waiting for a pat."

"They eat spaghetti in Italy," offered Albert.

"With chopsticks?"

"Gawd no. They twist it round their forks. There's a place in Italy called Pom-pay; they dug it out of a volcano—a whole town. There was bathrooms and kitchens complete—even loaves of bread still in the ovens."

Doris looked at her husband incredulously. "Go on; they'd be a bit stale."

"They were solid, you know, petrified. Pomp-pay is thousands of years old. I read it in the Digest."

He looked at the Italian as if for confirmation. "Pom-pay," he shouted. "He'll understand. Volcano, Pomp-pay."

The Italian looked delighted. "Compre, volcano, si."

"See, he understands," Albert looked benignly on the Italian who was now holding his hand to his stomach.

"Si, volcano; capisco, capisco!"

"I reckon I'll have him talkin' English in a couple of weeks," Albert said.

"Or you talking Italian." Doris began to pack the dishes together. At the sink the Italian joined her, tea towel in hand.

"Per favore," he said. "Permisso." The even teeth as white as piano keys in the pink gums.

"Here no." Albert grumbled from the table. "Hey Iti', that's woman's work."

"He wants to help," Doris said.

"I'm supposed to be payin' him for fencing, not dishwashing." Albert's face disappeared behind the paper.

Doris glared back at him. Her hands trembled on the saucepan as she felt her anger mounting. Then remembering their visitor she forced her attention back to the sink. But too late not to catch the Italian's eye and his swift sympathetic downward glance that took in the fullness of her nursing breasts. She blushed slightly and hastily turned on the hot water tap...

Perhaps that was the time when it all began. The caroling of magpies in the nearby trees, always a sound of home, became the moment of the Italian's acceptance. This was the strange country's atmosphere. Black and white birds warbling in gum blossoms. The cicadas stirring the garden shrubs in the heavy heat of midday. He must have heard them also, taken it in, realized the enormity of his foreignness in such a country, so far, so soundful, so scentful of gums and wattle brush and the smoke from the surrounding, harboring hills...

She had watched him, the days after, coming and going, his small tight body almost bursting with an unsatisfied energy. Helping her, being kind, learning words, accepting Albert's coarseness with unperturbed indifference, touching the baby delicately on the head as he passed. More often now, coming closer to brush her arm or touch her fingers.

He came in once and accidentally caught her feeding the baby, his eyes for a moment devoured the white cornucopia of her breast. Was he embarrassed? It was hard to say. The baby catching his movement, looked up solemn-eyed and wavered on puppet neck. When it hiccuped Doris laughed and she did not hurry to pull the cardigan across the tan-red starkly rising nipple of her corpulent breast...

Doris forgot the incident and Albert, reading on through the pregnant silences of each evening, noticed nothing. Uncaring. Shouting pidgin English. Cursing and finally snoring, feet up, boots scratching and defacing the hard polished agony of keeping clean—keeping nice—being houseproud. Never knowing of Doris's dreaming of oranges in Sorrento. Doris being stimulated by the places she had never seen. Doris longing for something through the long warm days and not knowing what it was she longed for...

Albert, who didn't know either, left for town, for the weekend to see the wool sold. To have an excuse to meet up with the boys, yarn, shout, get drunk, hog mutton chops. Perhaps to whore along the waterfront pubs and alleys. To steal the sailors' girls when the sailors were away at sea. So he went with a grimace for a smile, a smirk for getting away legitimately; blue-suited and sweating, he disappeared down the long dust-spewed lane and over the hill. Too dull, too insensitive to have seen the rekindled beauty and expectations of his wife dreaming of the youth that had escaped her. Vulnerable again as she was when a virgin in school.

Doris and the Italian remained behind and when the child was fed and hidden, over-ripe, beneath the mosquito net, they lay on the bed and made love. Exhilarated, encouraged and chorused by the magpies, who in their high world of red-tipped gums and crackling summer heat, saw more and knew more, than any, or all of them...

For the first few days after Albert came back, Doris found herself guiltily searching his face for signs of suspicion. He must see the difference, or catch a glance between her and the Italian; an acknowledgment of the four days past was quite inevitable. She hesitated, her guilt and desires conflicting. She declined after a while even to speak to her dark, passionate lover. She even looked away when he, half-stripped, body gleaming with sun and water, washed in almost indecent pantomimic attitudes at the pump in the yard. She looked away to the trees in the old orchard, or to the mountain; seeking solace in the wonderful silences of her green and passionless surroundings.

But Albert the provider, the master, the pig; snored, yawned, scratched, sweated and waded through flood upon flood of platitudes. Blind, blatant offerings of nothing. Cloudy of mind and stuffed with stupidity, bleary as his pink-eyed sheep, he crashed into the built-in fences of his own words. She hated him for it; she hated his unjealous blunt egotistical personality. But most of all she hated his dreary love.

Sometimes she would awake at night feeling the warmth of the body beside her and it was all she could do to stop herself from reaching out to Albert, who was there, and not to her foreign lover. She lay awake, sometimes for hours, listening to the wind in the bush. Hearing a mopoke call from the barn. Hearing a dog whine; a door slam. She lay in her silence, wondering about right and wrong.

Albert snored peacefully beside her not knowing; and she his wife in name only, lay still, aching for sleep and staring at the ceiling, and in her sleep hoping to find, in dreaming, the Italian's Italy...

When Italy did come to her it was in a series of meager distorted pictures. Oranges in a Sorrento grove. The pink walls and sun-splashed ruins of ancient Rome. Somebody's son or daughter or Uncle Bill holding up a tower at Pisa. A golden new moon beach in a blue sea, a film star or a member of the Royal family, looking distinctly unroyal and uncomfortable in a Florida shirt and dark glasses, gazing down at her from a marble balcony. Dark, squat, characterless peasant women in head scarves standing by vineyards on a hill. A man and a donkey in a deserted village street. A glossy tinted woman's weekly view of the world, stirred with music, caressed with words, smelling of pomade, hair oil and bath soaps. Italy hidden in the foreign dark eyes of her lover. She longed to reach out and share his memories of home. To reconstruct her own limited pictures into something tangible and unblemished. She wanted to shake out the truth from her vague distorted dreaming...

"What is Italy like, Iti'—Vitorio?"

"Italia? Non capisco. I don't understanda."

"Where did you live?"

"Come? I am sorry."

"House?"

"Ah—si. Casa—house. Una casa in Santa Lucia—Napoli."

"What is Italy like Vitorio?"

"Like—ah, it is beauty—la bell' Italia!"

An agony of not knowing rose up in her. The simple words not really understood, fell about her, pointless and broken.

"I will go there someday Vitorio."

"Si."

"To Rome."

"Ah, Roma, si."

"I will throw coins in the fountain."

"I—do—not understanda."

"Ah, Vitorio—if only you could tell me—if only I could understand."

But did it matter after all, when being born down and taken ingloriously in the grass? Crucified in the bracken. Hearing her own birds, in her own trees and staring up into her own sky where the clouds moved in quickening rhythm.

The blueness engulfed her body and the ground beneath thrust her upwards; to heaven; to the stars; to a crescendo of silent, exploding ecstacy. Her naked and glistening lover poised aloft and now plummeting down to pinion her soulless body to the brown earth.

She lay surrendered in the invader's arms, on her own brown earth, in her own brown land...

For weeks—months, she now had no fear, no restrictions. When Albert was away; when he was asleep; when he wasn't looking. In and out of rooms, buildings, haylofts, banks of grass, hiding in the ferns. Dear God so undignified, so primitive, so painless, so easy—so easy. Perhaps pregnant, perhaps to be caught eventually—finally. Even hopefully. Sometimes wanting to shout out to her husband. "Here in the hay—here in the barn!"

Hay in her hair, hay fastening like dead yellow insects to the white of her thighs. The sweat gathering, running from her frenzied, twisting body, more alive even than those dead and gone excitements of first love. Her body, no longer controlled, had become a joy of sensuality.

Yet guiltily she started at the shock of a scuttering mouse. A wind that creaked the door. She promised herself that peace would come, someday. So she prayed for a peace silently for a peace she knew nothing of, to a God she knew even less...

He brought her a rose from the neglected garden—half wild and plum-red. He held the velvet petals up for her to smell. Offered it by her cheek.

"The same," he said, and put it in a glass of water.

At night he took out his mandolin. He caressed the polished bowl with his hands. He glanced to where the needles hesitated their acknowledgment. The music came, the words flowed. Strange words, strange songs from his foreign home. Each word for her, each note a fragment of love, unknown, yet familiar, a time, a place, a memory.

Albert looked up from behind his paper. His voice splitting the song in two. "You sure can sing Iti'. I reckon he's got a woman in town Doris. He sings all day and he sings all night. I think he's a bit of a ram in those tight jeans, eh Doris?"

He laughed coarsely and returned to his shroud of pipe smoke. His feet scraped the brick work.

"Anyway, I won't have to put up with it much longer," he said from the smoke. "When the rains come he'll be finished I reckon."

The needles stopped and Doris looked up. "Finished?"

"The fencing. No good paying someone to sit inside under yer feet all day..."

Awakening as the first drops fell. Hearing the unfamiliar sound of rain on the hollow roof above. Quietly slipping from the bed, leaving Albert snoring and muttering in his sleep. Across the yard, past the silent yellow-edged eyes of dogs; the rain gathering in the blackness above her already wetting her to the skin...

In his arms she lay again and listened to his words, his hands caressed her deeper and deeper. She waited for fulfillment as the rain roared on, heavier and heavier, into the night. It came from the hills, driving and roaring through the trees, shaking and tearing at the tin hut, till Doris thought they would be swept away and submerged by its fury. Then suddenly fading away, passing, leaving them, the wind shriek dying in the valleys.

"That was my love," Doris whispered in the dark. "My love is a storm..."

When she left his bed he reached out for her in half-sleep. The brown arm in the newly lit moon gleamed softly, curved now, and shaped with strength. A reassuring arm, Doris thought, an arm to lean on. Gently she placed it back under the sheet.

"You wait Vitorio," she said. "You wait, you'll see; tomorrow the sun will be shining."

But tomorrow it was raining; and the day after and the day after that...

Albert dropped the pen with a dramatic clatter.

"Five hundred and sixty dollars," he said, grimacing. He blew on the wet ink of the check. "Strewth, it's an expensive business."

He held on to it for a minute or so looking ruefully at it, and waived it back and forwards in front of the Italian's face.

Once the Italian reached for it, but it had fluttered out of his reach.

Albert smiled at the Italian's anxiety. "I suppose you'll go blowin' it on some sheila in town. You little dark blokes, yer get the women in."

"Give it to him for Christ sake," Doris felt herself close to screaming.

"Or-right, or-right." Albert handed the check over reluctantly. "It's a lot of money to spend with a bang."

"And five months is a long time to wait for it."

She thankfully watched the Italian tuck the money neatly in his shirt pocket. He smiled once; the end of the smile turning quickly to her.

"Good boy," he said. "Oi be seeing you." He put his coat on and walked out into the slow cold drizzle of rain.

"Look at him go," Albert said. "You'd think he'd got ants in his pants. A few quid in their pocket and they'll blow it." He shook his head wondering. "They ain't like us at all."

Doris looked anxiously towards the sudden roar of the engine. For a few seconds a great cloud of steam and smoke enveloped the Italian then the machine burst clear, careering directly towards the well. At the very last moment it spun away, raised itself on two wheels, hesitated and charged towards the gate.

Doris saw the Italian's one desperate wave over his shoulder before his disappeared down the lane.

"Stewth" Albert said. "Arrwiderchi." He went off in the opposite direction to the barn.

Doris listened to the sound of the engine fade in the distance. The light rain fell silently across the lucerne trees, coating them with a silver gossamer of dew. The only sound left now was the snapping of parrots beaks above her head. She looked up for a moment and watched the empty lucerne pods spinning to the ground. After a moment she became aware of the parrots, muttering to each other. Almost, Doris thought, as though they were gossiping...

"When's he goin' to come back," Doris said at tea.

Albert looked up from his soup, his spoon poised halfway to his mouth in mild astonishment. "He ain't," he said. The spoon dipped quickly to the soup.

Doris looked down at her trembling hands. "D'you mean to say he's just gone?"

"Why not?"

"What about his things?"

"What things?" Albert was only slightly interested.

"His clothes."

"Didn't have much. Chucked them in the side car I suppose."

Doris got up from the table heavily, her legs feeling helpless beneath her. "I thought—I mean he hardly said good-bye. I thought he was just goin' to town."

"So he was. I paid him up didn't I, every penny. More'n he was worth too, I reckon. He wasn't worth all *that* much..."

Doris sat on the stool by the sink, staring at the dirty dishes. Albert finished his tea; a moment notified by the scrape of his plate pushed away. He walked to the fire scratching himself and rubbing his stomach. He sat down heavily and burped.

"Ar, y'get sick of havin' somebody under yer feet all day. It's a pleasure not having to keep work up to him. I think I'll take a couple of days off. We'll take a trip to town—buy some clothes—see a picture p'haps." He put his feet up nosily, onto the mantelpiece. "I must admit though, old Iti' put in a good strainin' post. They'll be standin' long after we're all dead and gone."

"Yes." said Doris. "That's something."

Dead and gone. Was that the sound of an engine? Albert breathing heavily. Sound asleep. Uncaring.

Hearing a wind out of the trees, once heard before. A fluttering at the window. The invisible wind, a bird of night. What? Stopping many times, iron poised, arcing down, hesitating again. Listening, hopeful, never yet believing. Different from us? Yes, different, so different...The baby turning in its sleep, silence returning. Smiling fondly, forgetting, but the pain coming again. Words returning as if in a dream. Dreaming words. Hands detached, freckled, forgotten—not her hands. Remembering in the new life the strange broken pieces of the old. Listening again, in the lonely vast silence of her existence; then believing—

The memory at least was something to cling to, each night, each day; forever...

Geoffrey Dean, a compulsive writer with in excess of a hundred published stories, scripts and articles, "worked at all sorts of jobs simply because I didn't have a good education and consequently only certain jobs were available to me. As it turned out though, such experience I now consider invaluable." He went back to college and got his degree when he was past forty. In addition to his own writing, he now works part time for newspapers and film corporations..."according to my mood and financial desperation."

"I saw involvement looming and did not wish to be within the compass of the tentacles of that clinging octopus."

The Granny Room

BY JOHN HAYLOCK

I first met Mrs. Hayashi in London at the house of a friend who made regular business trips to Japan. I had been invited to meet her as I was about to take up a teaching post in Tokyo. "You must meet Mrs. Hayashi," Cuthbert Meade had said. "She can be of great help to you." And no sooner had I met her than she suggested that I should live in her house. Seeing what was probably an expression of doubt on my face (I have never been good at disguising my feelings) she said in passable English, "You have separate apartment. I just built one above my garage. It is for me when I am a widow and grandmother. I call it the 'granny room.' "

I raised my eyebrows. Mrs. Hayashi was *petite* and neatly dressed; she had a tidy head of jet hair above a face composed of small but well-defined features; her skin shone as if it had been polished; her eyebrows were carefully plucked, her lips subtly painted, her teeth, except for one gold incisor, perfect. An attractive woman. I wondered how old she was. She did not look old enough to be cast in the role of grandmother, and I knew her husband was alive as he was talking business to Cuthbert on the other side of the room. Mr. Hayashi could have been a grandfather, for he was gray and grizzled. I put his age at fifty-five, but Mrs. Hayashi did not seem a day over forty. I knew nothing of Japanese customs and supposed it was natural for a wife to be planning for her old age after her husband's demise while he was still living; however, I raised my eyebrows, and Mrs. Hayashi, sitting on the edge of Cuthbert's capacious sofa, leaned forward. "We rebuild our house, and so we think of future. My son twenty-two. Next year he will graduate. When he twenty-five he will marry."

"Has he a fiancée?"

"Not yet," replied Mrs. Hayashi. "It is not time now to find wife for him." Her small dark eyes flicked into mine and then down to examine the carpet. "At twenty-six my son will have a child."

"And you will be a grandmother." I nearly asked if she would have killed off her husband by then—only four years to go. Did Mr. Hayashi know of this plan? He must have been aware of it, for she could hardly have built the granny room without his knowledge. Anyway, four years was enough for me because my contract with the university was only for two.

Cuthbert's wife then joined us and the conversation moved from Japan to London. There were many questions I wanted to ask Mrs. Hayashi, but I did not have a chance to pose them as she turned to Mrs. Meade and began to bombard her, rather insistently, with queries about where to buy this and that. Where could she buy shoes, she asked, since her feet were so small? She looked down at them and giggled—was she proud of them? I was about to suggest that she go to the children's department at Selfridge's, but I rose instead, invented another engagement, said I would like to take her granny room, excused myself and left with her visiting card in my pocket.

That meeting with the Hayashis occurred towards the end of February. They were due back in Tokyo at the beginning of March and I arrived there in the middle of that month. I had let Mrs. Hayashi know of the day of my arrival, but not the flight number; I did not wish her to meet me since a professor from the university had promised to do that, and knowing from that brief meeting in Cuthbert's flat that she had a strong personality, I did not want her to steal the professor's thunder; and I was right, for Professor Naito was far from thunderous; modesty, courtesy and gentleness seemed to be his principal characteristics.

"You must be very tired," he said when I met him after emerging from the Customs' Hall at Narita Airport. He stood behind a fence with other welcomers and held on high a placard with my name on it. He was a dapper little man, whose iron-gray hair was long but neat, whose overcoat was well-cut, whose black shoes shone.

"It doesn't seem like four in the afternoon," I said. I had flown over the Pole from London, an exhausting eighteen-hour flight with one stop at Anchorage. "I hope my hotel is comfortable."

Professor Naito made no reply and put out a hand to help me with my suitcase.

"It's a lovely day," I remarked, observing the cloudless sky above the airport buildings while we were queuing for the "limousine" bus to Tokyo.

"Sometimes we have fine days in March, but not always."

I had got the airline to reserve a room for me in an expensive downtown hotel, because I had thought that three or four nights in international luxury would enable me to acclimatize myself gently to my new, exotic environment. I had informed Professor Naito of my plans and also that I would be living in Mrs. Hayashi's flat, because the good Professor had offered to find me accommodation.

The comfortable bus gently glided along the highway. I looked out at thickly wooded hills between which nestled fields and farmhouses with steep gray roofs. "How pretty!" I said.

"Soon dreadful Tokyo begins," replied the Professor.

He was right, for it was not long before an unmitigated mass of concrete molded into unoriginal shapes took over from the dark-green hills. Professor Naito explained that Mrs. Hayashi had contacted him and that she would be meeting us at the air terminal, and then added, "Frankly speaking, I have something to tell you which you may not like."

I braced myself for bad news. Had my appointment been

canceled? Had discoveries been made about my past? "Yes," I replied, "please tell me." I supposed that the university, which had paid my fare, would provide me with a ticket home.

"It concerns Mrs. Hayashi," he said looking across me at a regiment of huge apartment blocks. How ugly Tokyo seemed! Would it all be like this, I wondered.

"Mrs. Hayashi?" I repeated the name.

"Yes. She will take you directly to the apartment she prepared for you."

"But I reserved a room in a hotel as I told you in my letter."

"She canceled the reservation." Professor Naito's dark eyes peeped at me; like a child's they were, gauging a grownup's reaction.

"Why should she do that? I wrote to her saying that I would move into her place after spending a few days in a hotel."

"Yes, yes, you told me. I fully understand your reasons, very wise ones. But Mrs. Hayashi, well, she wanted to save you the expense of—"

"I see. Well, never mind. I suppose she meant to be kind." I omitted to add that her meddling annoyed me because I did not want to upset Professor Naito, who seemed infinitely kind and solicitous.

"That is all right then," he said with relief. "I shall leave you at the terminal after I have put you into Mrs. Hayashi's capable hands."

Was I right in sensing that the arrangements for me to go directly to Mrs. Hayashi's and not first to a hotel suited Professor Naito too? It meant that he could give up shepherding me; but perhaps I was being unfair. The bus crossed a brown river, a recorded female voice made a long announcement in Japanese through the loudspeakers, and then another female voice in an overprecise accent mouthed (I could almost see her mouthing) in English the information that we would shortly arrive at Tokyo City Terminal, where we would find taxis and buses for our onward transportation. The bus extracted itself from the tangle of vehicles on the highway and entered a walled ramp and then ascended to the "ter-min-al beeldeeng." Professor Naito and I descended two flights of moving stairs to the baggage hall, where Mrs. Hayashi awaited us.

She looked broader, less slight than she had done in London; this was perhaps because of her fur coat, which she wore open. She greeted me cordially rather than warmly (there was not much warmth in her), shaking my hand; she bowed deeply to Professor Naito, who bent even lower towards her. After this little pause for the showing of mutual respect, the three of us joined the line for taxis with my suitcase, which the Professor had insisted on collecting for me from the revolving band in the luggage hall. Mrs. Hayashi made conventional inquiries about my health, the flight, my impressions of Tokyo, in less accurate but more fluent English than Mr. Naito's. When we reached the head of the queue, the Professor obsequiously helped Mrs. Hayashi and me into a taxi and then stood back and waggled an open hand. "Aren't you coming with us?" I asked, but by then the door had shut on its own and we were away. "How did the door shut?"

"The driver. It is automatic," explained Mrs. Hayashi. "We are now going to pass through the center of Tokyo to the district where you are going to live."

It was dark by this time and except for the ideographic signs that were appropriately exotic to me, the streets, the lights, the building and the traffic did not bear many startling marks of difference from those of any other city I knew, and the fact that one drove on the left made me feel less abroad. After half an hour or so of stopping at lights and then moving slowly on, we crossed a park. "Our B.B.C.," said Mrs. Hayashi, pointing out a solitary block, the sides of which were striped with fluorescent light. "And this is Yoyogi Park."

"Yoyogi?" I repeated the name, which sounded funny and reminded me of a toy I played with in my boyhood. "I remember Yo-Yo's," I said.

"Yo-Yo's?" She did not seem to understand and I was too tired to explain. We crossed several more traffic lights and then my companion began to give instructions to the driver, who turned into a narrow road, then left, then left again and up a hedged lane which in the dark seemed countrified. "Here we are," cried Mrs. Hayashi. "You see it's quite central."

"Yes," I replied, but I did not then see that it was central.

"This is the house," she declared, after she had paid the taxi-driver (she brushed aside my feeble fumblings with the strange money I had brought from my bank in England) and I had got my suitcase out of the boot. I looked up at a concrete slab of a house, standing sideways on to the road.

"Your flat—the granny room—is up there." She indicated a flight of iron steps flanked by iron railings which led up to a door above a garage that housed a car around which junk was stacked: boxes, a kitchen range, two rusty bicycles—the kinds of things whose uselessness is not accepted by a parsimonious owner. "Leave your suitcase here by the car. No one take it. We go up to your room after dinner." I followed my landlady down a passage to the front door of her house. "You must take off your shoes and put on these slippers," she commanded when she had opened the door with her key, and stepped up into the hall from the well by the entrace. "It's our custom as you probably know, and," she added rather severely, "one most foreigners like. Well, welcome to my home!" She took off her fur coat and in a petulant tone called up the stairs. "Nori-chan! Nori!" There was no answer. "My son seems to be out. Or he may be asleep."

Mrs. Hayashi was wearing a bottle-green woolen dress with a thick black suede belt tight round her tiny waist; her breasts were barely noticeable, and her fingers were ringless. I was shown into a sitting-room that was dominated by a gigantic stereo set and speakers—"My husband's," she said, giving the machine a derogatory wave. "Please sit down." I sat in a leather armchair, one in which Mrs. Hayashi would be lost; she perched on its companion for a moment, rather a restless moment, and then, excusing herself, left the room hurriedly. On each side of the stereo set was a tall bookcase: one held a number of Japanese tomes and the other a collection of ornaments and dolls, none of which seemed of much value. At the end of the room were sliding glass doors which gave on to an umbrageous garden lit in a ghostly fashion by the crude light of a fluorescent street lamp. I got up and with my nose nearly rubbing the glass looked at the shrubs and the trees; I hoped there would be a view of them from my room. Mrs. Hayashi reappeared. She said, "My garden," and then took me into a spacious kitchen in the middle of which was a dining-table covered with a plastic cloth; round the table were four bulky dining-chairs with arms and cushioned seats. I sat opposite my hostess and facing a row of up-to-date kitchen appliances: a refrigerator, a deep-freeze, a sink and a range; behind me were cupboards tidily stacked with crockery. The room was as neat and clean as Mrs. Hayashi.

I felt like a surrogate husband—was that part of her plan. Did she have designs on me? We had *sukiyaki,* a cook-it-yourself dish, which I was to learn is often served by Japanese to foreigners. Deftly manipulating a pair of long chopsticks, Mrs. Hayashi put into a pan on top of a gas ring placed on the table slivers of beef and shreds of cabbage, a kind of vermicelli, floppy-headed mushrooms and some sake from a little porcelain decanter. She served me saké too into a tiny china cup, instructing me to hold the cup towards her while she poured.

As I clumsily helped myself from the pan with my chopsticks, occasionally letting fall a piece of meat, a mushroom, I re-examined Mrs. Hayashi's face. I decided that the thoughts I had had about her in London were right: she was an attractive woman. It was a pity about her gold incisor as her other teeth were good; but otherwise her tidy hair, her tidy face were impressive; tidy was the best word to describe her features, which, with her trim eyebrows, her neat nose, lips a sculpture could not have improved upon, were compact, like a new set of tools in a case. Her dark eyes were small, and though bright they shone with what seemed to be a forced brightness, and were kept puckered at their inner corners; perhaps her chin and her eyes betrayed her strong character. Good-looking, yes, undoubtedly good-looking, yet somehow she lacked appeal—at least to me: this was due to her manner, which was not at all soft and feminine. Was she the decision-maker in the family? Did she wear the trousers? I had scarcely met Mr. Hayashi, only having shaken hands with him at Cuthbert's in London. I remembered him as a little man with thick, gray hair and dark-rimmed spectacles—that was all I remembered about him. Where was he now? It was nearly half-past eight. Was he away? Should I ask? I was just about to inquire when my hostess said, "Are you tired?"

"Well, I am, rather," I said. I was longing for a whisky. I did not much care for the tepid rice wine and I yearned to get out my duty-free bottle and pour myself a treble. "The flight over the Pole takes eighteen hours," I said.

"Yes," Mrs. Hayashi replied. "I find coming West-East not so tiring as coming East-West. Here the time"—she looked at her little silver wrist-watch—"eight-twenty-eight and so in England it is about eleven-thirty in the morning, so your day finished and when you go to bed most of your day missed. From here to London you have to have the day again, so West-East less tiring."

I did not quite follow her reasoning, but I realized from her speech that I was not expected to be tired.

After I had eaten as much of the *sukiyaki* as I wanted—the beef was delicious—I was served a bowl of clear soup with a tiny egg floating in it and finally a crême caramel in a plastic cup—the last obviously bought. Then Mrs. Hayashi rose. I also got up. "We go to your room," she announced. Was it only a room? And out of the house we went, she carrying, in a fussy way that suggested she was doing something extra, my plastic bag of duty-free drink and cigarettes, my briefcase and my overcoat, and behind her I lugged my suitcase up the iron steps.

The "room" was more than a room, two rooms in fact, and there was a bathroom also, off the bedroom, which had in it a three-quarters double-bed, a "honeymooner" as some call it. The disadvantage about the sitting-room, I noticed at once, was the kitchen, which was in an unventilated alcove at the back of the room. Mrs. Hayashi went proudly to the window (the curtains were undrawn) and exclaimed, "The garden, you see? You look on my garden. We call this *shakkei,* borrowed view. So," she went on, gazing into a reflection of herself in the glass, "when I live here I not lose my garden."

I smiled wanly. I was pleased with the flat, which was adequately furnished with a carpet, a sofa, armchairs, a desk and a dining-table. It was clear that she had carefully considered the needs of a Westerner. "Of course," she said, "I like better *tatami,* Japanese mats, to a carpet, and a cushion to a chair. When I live here I have *tatami* put down." She talked as if her moving in were imminent. Was her son about to marry? Was a grandchild on the way? What about her husband? Had she got rid of him? I decided I must ask. "Is your husband away?"

"He at work," she replied, rather sharply.

"And your son?"

"Nori is out. Well, it getting late. We will talk about contract for apartment in the morning."

I slept well in the "honeymooner" and I was pleased to find all the ingredients necessary for breakfast in the refrigerator. Mrs. Hayashi had even remembered marmalade. How practical she was! How businesslike too! For soon after breakfast, before I had telephoned Professor Naito, she arrived with the contract for the flat. "The rent is one hundred thousand yen a month; this reasonable for this district." Two hundred pounds a month seemed a lot for two rooms, one of which was partly a kitchen, but I could only accept. I signed and agreed to arrange for my bank to pay the rent on the twenty-eighth day of each month. After neatly folding her copy of the contract, Mrs. Hayashi said, "You may think rent high?" My face as usual had shown my feelings. "I do not ask key money or rent in advance, and if you are willing to give Nori English lessons two times a week, I pay you thirty thousand yen a month."

I agreed. I had to be at the university on only three days in the week, so could easily fit in lessons for Mrs. Hayashi's son, and £60 a month seemed a fair fee. "What year is he in at his university?"

"He a senior. His major economics."

I was not used to these American terms, but did not then inquire into their precise meaning. "I can't teach him economics," I said.

"No. You teach him English. I want him speak English good."

Shortly afterwards I bravely introduced myself to the mysteries of the Tokyo subway system, going to the local station down a pleasant hedged lane of azalea bushes and a narrow shopping-street which was excitingly strange, with its shops all open at the front, their wares on display, its wooden houses and small blocks of flats, tiny bars and little restaurants. I met Naito at a central station and he conducted me to the university, where I shook hands with a number of professors (everyone seemed to be a professor), who were very cordial. The term was not to begin for two weeks. When I returned to my flat, I found a note from Mrs. Hayashi on my desk. The fact that she had a key and could let herself in while I was out (or even when I was in) disturbed me a little. The note said that she would be bringing her son to see me at eight and I was to let her know only if this was not convenient.

At eight precisely my two-tone doorbell sounded and I let in Mrs. Hayashi and Nori. The young man, who stood head and shoulders above his mother, had a longish face and black wiry hair that covered his ears, and the back of his shirt collar was outside his light-blue pullover, which was more or less the same color as his jeans. "Here is my son," said Mrs. Hayashi. I held out my hand, but the son, very solemn, bowed, putting his hands on his thighs; when he looked up I saw he had a brown and healthy complexion, and his smile was more generous and warmer than that of his mother, who never allowed her lips to expand fully. When they had sat down I said, "I have only whisky to offer you, I'm afraid."

"No, thank you," said the mother, "we do not want drink anything."

By the expression in Nori's large dark eyes I guessed he would have liked a glass of whisky, but I did not dare give him one. We talked, or rather Mrs. Hayashi held forth about her son, saying that his English was very poor, that he did no work at the university, that he was out most nights. Nori looked down at his folded hands during the string of complaints. What was I to say? I did not want to side with the mother, for that might have started off the teacher-pupil relationship on the wrong track, so I simply interpolated an "Oh?" now and then. Mrs. Hayashi rose. "I hope you make Nori into a good English speaker," she said and departed, leaving her son behind; it seemed that she expected him to be speaking perfect English by the time he returned to the house next door.

Nori was shy and said very little. Obviously I had to win his confidence somehow and I was not sure how to do this. After receiving monosyllabic answers to my stock questions about age, study and recreation—"Do you like reading?" "Yes." "Have you read any English books?" "Yes." "What books have you read?" "*The Catcher in the Rye.*" "Did you like it?" "Yes,"—I decided that a little whisky might help. It did. After a second whisky, Nori talked freely and with surprising frankness about his mother. "My mother expects much of me," he said. "She want me enter Tokyo University, but I fell extrance examination and was *ronin* for one year. She very angry. Tokyo University very high standing and students from there get good jobs, certain. Now I am student at private university. Not so good. My mother want me go to Tokyo University and join some Ministry, maybe Finance Ministry and then later become Prime Minister." I smiled, but the young man was quite serious.

"What does *ronin* mean? And I think you meant 'failed' not 'fell'—and 'entrance' not 'extrance'."

"Yes, sorry, failed. *Ronin* student who failed university entrance examination and must study until next year examination. He has no school, no university. *Ronin* in old Japan was *samurai*—you know *samurai?*" I nodded. "Ronin was *samurai* without his lord. Maybe the lord lose his land and so his *samurai* must go away and wander."

"I see; rather a good expression. Do you want to read a book with me when you come for your lessons, or just talk?"

"As you like."

"I think we'd better read a book. It would give us something to talk about, be a basis for our conversations."

"O.K. What we read?"

"Let's decide later. I'll see what there is available. What about your father? What did he say when you failed to get into Tokyo University?"

"He no say much. He went to small university. It was just after war end. Very different then. He has his own company. Very busy. Always very busy." Nori put some resentment into the last three words.

It was at the fourth lesson—we had chosen to read a book of stories by Somerset Maugham—that Nori said, when I asked him a question about "Rain" which he could not answer, "I am in love."

"Oh? Who with?"

"A hairdresser."

"What sort of hairdresser?"

"She is thirty-two years old and married and has two children, two girls."

"Oh dear!"

"Her husband not live with her. Leave her. She live with her mother. Her father dead."

"Where does she work?"

"She work near the station."

"The station near here?"

"Yes. My mother go her shop. She cut her hair and give it perm sometimes."

"How fascinating! Does your mother know of your connection with this hairdresser?"

"She not know."

"Perhaps we should read a little of 'Rain'?"

Nori made a *moue*, but I reminded myself that I was being paid for the lesson and we read a little of "Rain." Nori's mind, though, was not on the story at all. "What are you going to do about her?" I asked.

"What can I do?"

"Do you see her often?"

"Yes, but it is difficult. I cannot tell my mother. Girlfriend work very near. I pass her shop every day when I go my university. I look in. Sometime she see me; sometime she busy."

"When do you meet her?"

"After her work, we meet. Not near here. It is dangerous near here. People they know me; all my life I live here."

"Does she love you?" This was an impertinent question, but I was curious to know the answer.

"Yes, she love me," replied Nori with certainty. "Once we go together to Hakone, near Mount Fuji and..." Instead of finishing his sentence, he said, "It is very difficult. What you think should I do?"

"I don't know. I see nothing wrong with your having an affair with her." Nori's eyes brightened; he clearly wanted approval. "But," I went on, hoping to dilute the encouragement I had given him, "don't go too far. She's much older than you and it may be hard for her to find a husband, so don't become too attached to her."

"I love her."

"Yes—love. But that is not enough," I said, silently upbraiding myself for my sententiousness. "Go carefully, I shouldn't be advising you. But think of your mother and don't do anything hasty. Perhaps you should tell your mother."

Nori turned down his mouth at my last suggestion, which I realized was unhelpful; he probably felt that I, being about his mother's age, sympathized with her. "You not tell her?"

"No. I won't. It's not my business."

I am inquisitive by nature, a despicable characteristic, but a human and forgivable one nevertheless, and so after Nori had told me his story my walk to the station became more interesting. There were two hairdressers in the little shopping-street, one on the right at the top and the other on the left at the bottom near the railway line. I wondered in which one Nori's lover worked. The sex of the hairdressers or stylists or trichologists was not easy to determine through the windows of the shops, but I gathered that some were women and others men. I guess that Nori's mistress belonged to the shop that had on its window the words "Spring up your Hair" (it was now April and Mrs. Hayashi's cherry tree had bloomed and come into leaf) and not to the one called "Beauty Style," for the former looked the more prosperous of the two and had five chairs to the other's three.

Nori often stayed away from his lessons and I was not sure whether I should tell his mother about this. I decided not to because I was beginning to feel sorry for him. Why should the poor, wretched, mother-run boy not kick over the traces a bit with a hairdresser before becoming harnassed to a job?

I rarely saw Mr. Hayashi. He had come up to my room one evening soon after my arrival and seemed rather tongue-tied; perhaps he was shy, so many Japanese men were, I was beginning to realize, for he did not say much except a polite "I hope you comfortable," and he refused a drink. After that we only passed the time of day on the rare occasions we saw each other going out or coming in. On Sunday mornings, pipe in mouth and wearing a little round cloth hat, he would mow the lawn, but although I could see him from my window I never tossed out a "Nice day!" or "I'm enjoying your roses," for I felt that I should not disturb his privacy, and if he wanted to see me he could easily come up to the granny room; on Sunday afternoons, Beethoven, usually the "Emperor," boomed into the garden from the sitting-room below, and once I greeted him with a "So you like Beethoven?" But all he answered was, "Beethoven? Oh, yes. Beethoven," and this made me suspect that he was more concerned with the performance of his stereo set than with the music. Mrs.

Hayashi often rang my bell and inquired if I needed anything. This was kind of her, but I found her attention rather intrusive; after all, one wants to see one's landlady only when the plumbing has gone wrong, the geyser has broken or the roof is leaking. One day Mrs. Hayashi called when Nori should have been with me having a lesson.

"Is Nori with you?" she asked at the door. She rarely came into my flat. I think this was because the taking off of shoes and the putting on of slippers commit one to a proper visit, as it were. When I replied that Nori had not turned up, Mrs. Hayashi stepped out of her shoes and into a pair of slippers in two quick, almost imperceptible, movements. I ushered her into the sitting-room and into a chair from which the kitchen range could not be seen. On the stove was one of my attempts to make a *daube* and I did not want any comments or any advice.

"Is this the first time he not come to his lesson?" she inquired.

I hesitated for a moment or two, wondering whether I should reply honestly, and then I did. "No," I said, "it's not the first time."

"Why you not tell me?"

This time I did not reveal what I truly thought, which was that she ought to allow her son, who had come of age, to decide for himself whether he wanted a lesson or not. "I didn't think that it mattered all that much," I replied. "I presumed that he was busy with some university activity; he's no longer a schoolboy." I had never imagined for one moment that he sacrificed trysts with his hairdresser-lover for some academic chore, but I was on his side. I had not warmed to Mrs. Hayashi, and I have always supported rash, passionate youth against the opposing forces of age, experience, reason and sanity. I have frequently iterated to students a "gather-ye-rosebuds-while-ye-may" philosophy, because I really believe that in the world of woe in which we live happiness, even self-indulgent, sensual pleasure, should be snatched when offered. So I approve of Herrick's advice "To Virgins, to make much of Time," but of course Mrs. Hayashi would abhor the poet's "That age is best, which is the first..."

The interview with Mrs. Hayashi did not last long; possibly she sensed my antipathy to her great "plan for Nori." She sipped only twice from the cup of Earl Grey I poured out for her, and broke delicately in two a chocolate biscuit which was small enough to put whole into the mouth, even into her tiny one, and ate only one half. She left me, her almost full cup of tea, and the other half of the biscuit, saying, "Thank you very much for the nice cup of tea and the cookie. Very delicious." I saw her to the door and she repeated her thanks, but her eyes looked down, not into mine.

June arrived; the pink and red azalea blooms were succeeded by the pale blue and purple clusters of the hydrangeas; the notice on the window of the second hairdresser's shop was changed to, "Fresh up Gals with Summer Hair." I did not yet know which of the assistants had stolen Nori's heart, though he had told me that *she* worked in the shop near the station. We had not progressed very much with "Rain" in spite of the fact that the appeal of the story had increased by the arrival of the rainy season, for Nori only wanted to talk about his love. About Mrs. Davidson, the missionary's wife in the story, he once remarked, "She like my mother." I was tempted to try to engage his interest by suggesting that Sadie Thompson and his lady hairdresser might have something in common, but I did not do so through fear of hurting his feelings. He was very sensitive and was not a person would could laugh at himself or at his predicament.

One evening—our lessons were supposed to last from five until six-thirty, though Nori never turned up before five-thirty—he said, "Her name is Keiko—I want to introduce you."

"Oh, why?"

"I want you tell me what you think."

I saw involvement looming and did not wish to be within the compass of the tentacles of that clinging octopus. "I don't think my advice would be of much help."

"Please."

"I won't be able to speak to her."

"You can judge by seeing."

"Where could we meet?" I was of course curious to know what this thirty-two-year-old divorcee-hairdresser with two daughters was like.

"Outside Isetan Department Store in Shinjuku. You know?"

"Yes, when?"

"Tomorrow, eight o'clock p.m."

I agreed.

Naturally, I had speculated much upon the physiognomy and the character of Nori's beloved and I had decided that she was one of the "fluffy" girls I had espied through the window of the Ladies' Hairdresser's near the station, one of the girls whose hair had been dyed copper and fuzzed into a bush of tight curls. I was quite wrong.

I met Nori outside the department store and he took me across the street into a building that housed several small cinemas and up in a lift to a café called "Mozart"—an old-style café with straw-seated, wooden chairs with hooped backs, which served *Kaffee mit Schlag* and creamy *Torte;* the background music was exclusively that of the Austrian composer, of whom there was a bust on the cake-counter. Nori led me to a table at which was sitting a woman who was mature in a motherly way that Mrs. Hayashi was not. Keiko had a shiny head of black, straight hair that danced over her forehead and her ears, and a figure that was full rather than fat. Her pale-white skin accentuated the darkness of her hair, her eyebrows and her eyes. She had a round face and a largish mouth that turned up at the corners when she smiled. She exuded a womanly warmth and a protectiveness that were obviously captivating to an inexperienced young man; and it was clear by the way she kept looking at Nori when he spoke that she was in love with him.

The meeting did not extend much beyond the time it took to drink a cup of coffee and eat a cake. I did not know what to say and Keiko could speak no English. Nori told me about the café being dedicated to Mozart—the place was nearly empty but it was near closing-time—and we had a desultory conversation about this and that—about how I liked Japan and so on. I was relieved when the young man said, "It getting late" and we left. In the street, we bade each other good-night and parted. I went back to the granny room next door to Nori's home, but he did not accompany me; he went off with Keiko.

One evening a few days later Nori burst into my room—he knew that I never locked the door. I pulled myself up from my prostrate, post-prandial posture on the sofa, half-gathered together my somnolent wits and said, "Oh, hello?"

When I had got him a whisky and one for myself (I do not usually drink after dinner but his arrival gave me an excuse to do so), he said, "We're going to 'erope.' "

I thought he meant Europe. "But how? It's term time. You can't get away. You mustn't give up your studies. And what about money?"

"I get *arbeit*."

"In Germany?"

"Germany? Why you say Germany?"

"But you say you're going to Europe and—"

"Not Europe—'erope.' "

I then realized that Nori meant "elope." He explained that *arbeit* was used in Japan to mean a part-time job.

"So you will leave home?"

"Yes."

"What will your mother say?"

"I not tell her. I just go." Nori looked at me, his dark eyes wide, liquid, pleading. "Will you do something for me?"

"What?"

"You tell my mother about my going. You tell my mother you meet Keiko-san and that she is very nice girl."

"You want *me* to tell your—"

"My mother she like you very much; if you tell her she not be angry with you. So you tell her, please."

"No, you must tell her."

"I can't."

"It's none of my business. It is your family affair. It's nothing to do with me." There was alarm in my voice as I spoke, alarm that betrayed weakness, which Nori detected, I'm sure; he had some of his mother's forcefulness.

"So you tell her. Tell her tomorrow. I will go to Keiko tonight."

"Where? Where will you go?"

"To a room we rented."

"What about her children?" I threw this question at him, hoping it might make him reconsider his plan.

"They stay with her mother."

"Why do you decide to do this? Why not carry on as you have been doing?" I knew these were silly questions, for if one is young and in love one wants to be with one's lover as much as possible. Nori's answer was a simple, "I can't." I followed him to the door, where he trod into a pair of grubby gym-shoes with broken backs and took up a bulging grip which he had left in the entrance.

"Why not tell your mother now? It's much better for you to tell her."

"She in bed. Always she go to bed at nine-thirty."

"What about your father?"

"He on business trip. Good-bye. Thank you very much." He jerked a little half-bow, crept down the iron staircase and hastened round the corner out of sight.

What was I to do? I did not relish telling Mrs. Hayashi that her son had gone off to live "in a room" with a divorced hairdresser. The next day was a Wednesday, a day when I had to leave early for the university, and one on which, during the lunch-break, I invariably arranged to see Professor Naito. I decided not to give Nori's message to Mrs. Hayashi (the more I thought about it, the more monstrous I regarded his behavior—not so much his running away from home, but his involving me in his escapade) until the evening, after I had asked the kind professor his advice.

"May I come and see you at noon?" I asked him on the telephone from my room in the university, and in his usual deferential way, he replied, "I don't want to trouble you, I shall come to your room." When I answered his gentle taps on my door with a "Come in!" he entered apologetically, as if he were making an intrusion.

"I have a problem," I announced.

"Oh?" he said in a rising tone.

"It's to do with Mrs. Hayashi and her son Nori."

"Oh." The second "oh" was on a falling tone of relief. I think the professor feared that I was going to complain about teaching—or salary conditions. I then told him the story and how the selfish young man had landed me with the unenviable task of informing his mother of his flight.

Professor Naito asked, "Did you encourage Nori-san to go away with this woman?"

"No, of course I didn't." I did not say that I had not condemned the affair and that playing the role of confidant had amused me. "But what should I do?"

"You must tell her. He was your pupil, and as his teacher you have responsibility."

"I don't see that I have, Professor Naito. I am a foreigner here and—" An idea came to me "I wonder if I could ask you a favor."

"A favor?" He seemed uncertain.

"Could you come with me this evening when I tell Mrs. Hayashi? Apart from your deep knowledge of English—Mrs. Hayashi may have a good ear for the language, but she doesn't have a very big vocabulary—your moral support would be of enormous assistance."

Professor Naito looked very confused. "I am sorry to say that this evening there is a faculty meeting."

"Couldn't you miss it?"

"Not possible, I am sorry to say." Naito smiled.

"Then do you think you could telephone Mrs. Hayashi and tell her that I shall be calling on her about six, and give her the gist of what I've told you about her son? It would help prepare the ground if you did, and you could tell her in Japanese and therefore in the Japanese way, which would be so much better than the clumsy, Western way I would use."

Professor Naito looked at his watch. "I'll see," he replied. "It is a difficult matter."

I guessed this meant that he would not telephone, and I was right; for when I rang Mrs. Hayashi's two-tone bell she came to the door in an apron over a white blouse and black trousers and welcomed me in her usual way with a flash of her gold incisor and a businesslike, "How *are* you?" She must have noticed from my expression that something was amiss, for she said, "You not well?" And when I said I was all right, she asked me if anything had gone wrong with the granny room, as indeed it had in a way, on the "granny" side of it, at least. "The water heater again broken?" It had failed to function three times since my arrival and Mrs. Hayashi had telephoned a mechanic who had come after an annoying delay of several days. I did not know whether I should ask to come into her house to impart my news, to invite her upstairs to the granny room, or to blurt out about the wayward son on his mother's doorstep. "It's about Nori," I said.

She did not grasp my meaning, for she said, "He is not here. He not come home last night. Probably he spend last night with one of his university friends. Sometimes he does. Is it his lesson day?"

"No, but he came to see me last night and told me that he was going away." I should have gone on and not allowed the strong-minded lady to speak before I had finished my message.

"Sometime he go away with a university friend. He live in Yokohama." She had not listened properly to what I had said.

"Nori asked me to tell you he was going away to live with his girl friend."

Mrs. Hayashi let out a humorless laugh. "It is his joke. He has not girl friend."

"But he has. I met her." As soon as I let the last words slip out I wished I had not done so, for now I was deeper in the plot than I had meant to be.

"You met her? Where?"

"In Shinjuku. And last night, very late, Nori came to see me and asked me to tell you he was going to live with her."

"Where?"

"I don't know. In a room. They have rented a room."

"Why he ask you to tell me this? Why he not tell me himself?" I was sure she must have an inkling to the true answer to this question, but I simply replied, "I don't know."

"I see."

I then excused myself and went up to the granny room, leaving her flummoxed at her own front door, and hoping that, as far as I was concerned, the affair was over. I was mistaken. After an hour or so my wretched two-tone bell tinkled and it was she. She had changed into a dress, a severe dark-blue one, which, I imagined, she had thought suitable for the occasion.

"I don't know what to say," she said when she had accepted a chair but refused a brandy. "You tell me that you know this girl friend of Nori-san?"

"Not know. I met her once, as I told you—er—in Shinjuku. I ran into Nori by chance and he was with her. He introduced me." Mrs. Hayashi was staring at me in astonishment, so, nervously, I continued. "She seemed nice, older than your son but very soft and feminine." I stopped myself from adding, "But you know her. She does your hair!"

"Soft and feminine?" Mrs. Hayashi repeated with distaste. "And how old?"

"I don't know; thirty, perhaps."

"Thirty? And married? Is she married?"

"I don't know." I thought it best to soften the blow a bit.

"What have you been teaching Nori?" she asked.

" 'Rain'—a story by Somerset Maugham."

"Some romantic stuff."

"Cynical, really."

"Some romatic stuff," she repeated. I don't think she understood the adjective I had used. "I know," she went on, "the romantic Western way. You teach that romance is good, that love is good." She was quite angry I felt, although her face did not show it.

"I haven't actually taught him that; but isn't love good?"

"No. Not this kind of passion love," replied Mrs. Hayashi, fervently. "He follow your way, your Western way. You responsible for this love affair he have with this woman."

"I don't think it's fair of you to blame me, Mrs. Hayashi. Nori is a man; he's twenty-two."

"Nori is a boy, a young boy, a young innocent boy."

"It won't harm him to lose his innocence. It will help him grow up. I'm sure this will soon blow over, Mrs. Hayashi, will pass; in a while he'll be home and right as rain."

"Is that what happens in the story?"

"No," I laughed; I could not help myself. " 'As right as rain' means 'all right.' "

"I don't think it is funny; for you perhaps it very funny; for me it is serious matter." She rose and said, "I leave you now." I saw her to the door and, without saying another word, she stepped out of her slippers, into her shoes and out of the granny room.

I did not see her or her husband for a week, and then my geyser broke down and I had to speak to her about it; but all she said when I asked her to call the mechanic was, "I see." Another week passed and no mechanic came. Then my air-cooler went wrong and I was very uncomfortable without it at night; but again all she said was, "I see," when I told her about it. A week went by, a week of sweaty nights, and days of boiling water in kettles and saucepans to have a bath and to wash up. I called on my landlady again, but all I got was another, "I see." I invoked the aid of Professor Naito and he advised me to move. "She wants you to go," he said. "She does not mend your equipments. That is the sign."

"I have a contract," I protested.

"Better to go," said Naito. "I will help you find other accommodations."

"No, thank you. I think I know of a place." I did not, but house agents advertised apartments almost every day in *The Japan Times,* and I decided to apply for a flat through one of them and not be beholden to Professor Naito in case things went awry again. Accommodation was found in the form of a flat that was more expensive, nosier, and with a far less attractive prospect than the granny room had—it was high up and looked on to another block—but the landlord dealt through the agent and never appeared himself. Mrs. Hayashi accepted my departure with equanimity. With her face closed, as if she had pulled a blind over it, she said, "Well, good-bye," when I summoned her to the door by pushing the hateful two-toned bell and handed her my key. I left on a day in late July when the white oleander was in flower and the myrtle tree was about to blush. "I shall miss your garden," I said, but she made no reply to this remark and kept the blind drawn.

In November, when the maple trees began to glow like embers, I felt the need of my overcoat, which, after a search, I realized I had left behind in the granny room. Several days of wondering what I should say to Mrs. Hayashi passed before I steeled myself into telephoning her. Without any preliminary politenesses I simply stated who I was and asked about my coat. "Yes it in the apartment," she replied. "Why don't you go there and ask for it? Someone is there."

"All right, thank you. Any news of—" But she rang off before I had time to say her son's name. When I called at the granny room there came to the door an American blonde with blue-saucer eyes, dressed in a turtle-neck pullover and jeans and with a cigarette in her mouth.

"I've come for my coat. Did Mrs. Hayashi tell you?" I could hear the squawks of children inside the flat.

"Yeah, sure. Why don't you come in?"

I followed the young mother into what used to be my sitting-room. Two unbashful, tow-haired tots glared at me for a moment and then went on playing with some model cars. "Make yourself at home," sang the Amercan lady, "and I'll see if I can find your coat. It's a top-coat, isn't it?"

"Yes. Gray mohair." I ignored the children because my eyes were drawn to the window by two dazzling maples outside. "How splendid the leaves are, aren't they?" I said to the American mother when she came in from the bedroom with my overcoat on her arm.

"Yeah. I'm just crazy about them." She, busy housewife that she was, took her cigarette out of her mouth and turned to her children. "Now I thought I told you, Chester, not to do that to your sister."

"D'you see much of Mrs. Hayashi?"

"Yeah, sure. She's really great. She comes up to baby-sit when Bill and I want to go out, and she doesn't charge a cent. She just adores the kids. You'd think she was their grandmother, really you would."

"Do you know what's happened to her son?"

"Son? I didn't know she had a son. She's never mentioned a son to me."

The widely-traveled John Haylock, currently teaching at a university in Japan, writes short stories, novels and articles. Best known in Great Britain, Mr. Haylock's writing reflects the breadth of his travels. He last appeared in SSI No. 27 with "Romance Trip."

"My body as you know, my dear,
is not strong enough to bear beating."

Dear Truth

BY ALI SHALASH

Torah Detention Camp
January 3rd, 1968

Dear Truth,

I owe you a very sincere apology for disturbing your peace, but I had no choice. Ten months or more have passed since I first thought of writing to you. I kept feeling afraid of writing lest I should be punished, for writing is forbidden at the place where I stay. Paper and pen were banned, but in time they appeared by means of smuggling, and then I began to feel eager to write. I said to myself: Why should I intrude upon your realm? Finally, after such long months of pain and suffering, I dared to hold the pen. Once again I apologize for writing down my words without much care or beauty.

Do you know, my dear, what I am doing at the moment in order to write? I am lying flat on my face with a black blanket underneath. The blanket is threefold and stretched on an asphalt floor to protect me from the severe cold of January. As for the three other blankets I am allowed, I have hung them a while ago to be freshened by the sun in the yard of the detention camp. The place where I am sitting, sorry, I mean lying flat on my face, is a rather long oblong made of stone, ten meters long and five meters wide, with a population of 50 men of different ages and ideologies. No one has chosen the other, rather, co-existence has been imposed on all.

Would you believe, my dear, that I have been tortured and caned like a child, in spite of my moustache; all because of you? Moreover, would you believe that I was kidnapped from my house and put in a tiny cell lit by electricity all day and all night, and then dismissed from my job and sent to the bottom of the social ladder? All for the sake of your eyes. Yes, do not laugh at me, for you should know. And this, unfortunately is exactly what doubles my pain; I felt you so remote from me. Yet I will remind you of what happened, for you may excuse one of your faithful subjects, or you may rather withdraw the permit you have granted me to contact you.

It was the tenth of last March. I was on my way home from a visit to a friend. It was eight p.m. when I bought some foreign books and newspapers and took the bus. The journey took half an hour and I kept so busy reading that I nearly missed my stop. At the last moment I realized where we were, got off the bus and crossed the street to my house, with a carrier bag hanging from my hand. At the entrance of the building where I live I was stopped by a well-dressed young man.

"Excuse me, do you know which flat is Mr. S. Hamza's?" he said.

Quickly, I looked him over from head to foot, and said: "Yes, I know. It is I. Who are you?"

"My name is Nabil, from the Secret Service," he said, fixing his eyes on mine.

I looked at the young man examining him all over again and again; then with the innocence of a child and the hospitality of a villager I pointed to the stairs.

"Come along," I said.

"You come along with me," he said, pointing to the outer door, as if inviting me to dinner.

"Where to?" I asked.

"Just out. Let me take this carrier bag out to the car and I'll be back with you. O.K.?" he said with a movie-star smile.

I simply handed him the bag and the two of us walked out where a fancy American car was waiting in the dark under my balcony. Apart from the driver who did not look at us, there was another, shabby-looking young man who swiftly jumped out, took the bag, put it in the back seat and came towards me. Again the first man pointed to the building's door, and the three of us marched back, like in a funeral, one to my right and one to my left. With a distracted mind I walked amidst the two young bodyguards.

"Now we are to search your flat," the first young man said, breaking the silence.

"What for?" I said.

"According to the orders, we have to search your flat and then we go together to the headquarters downtown, just for five minutes. O.K.?" he said with a smile.

I fell into complete silence and a cold calm took hold of me, but I kept wondering: what was it? Images of people hunted down by the Secret Service passed through my mind. I even remembered a friend of mine who worked at the Presidency; he would be of some benefit now. I mentioned his name to the first young man but he said there was no need for that. The whole thing would be finished within five minutes. I believed him without arguing. I wanted to believe him.

As we mounted the stairs I asked him not to disturb my mother, sisters and brothers who stayed with me, for they had never been to a police station, and it would be a great shock for them to see their supporter in such trouble; he willingly promised to do so.

As soon as I rang the bell, one of my sisters opened the door. I made a gesture to make her feel that I had some friends, asked her for three cups of coffee, and giving way to my guests they went into my room.

The search did not last long. The first young man asked me to open my drawers and searched through them for a while till he got hold of some pictures, letters and newspaper cuttings; the other looked over the titles on the bookshelves, while I turned on some music to hide any noise. When the coffee came they swallowed the contents of the small cups in one gulp, then looked at me.

"Thank you. Let us go in order not to keep you for long," said the first young man seriously.

I opened the door, turned the music off, and went out escorted as before, noticing that no one in the flat suspected anything.

As soon as I had been seated in the car, in between the two, the driver put his foot down on the gas as if he had to catch a plane at the nearby Cairo airport.

I wondered what I had done. Perhaps it had to do with the bookshop where I bought the books and newspapers; perhaps they were banned or something, but I was sure that the whole thing must be connected with some political activity. These two guards did not deal with civil affairs. They kept silent and I kept struggling to find out what it was...

My thoughts were interrupted by the car's abrupt halt. I looked out. It was the District Police Station. The first young man opened the door and asked me to join him, and the other hurried after us from the other side. We stepped out and walked in till we got into an empty office. He asked me to take a seat and reached for the telephone. I heard him talking about me in an indirect way. I gathered from what he said that he wanted to reassure the one on the phone of my surrender and that we were on the way to him. He glanced at me and left. I looked at the other; neither of us said a word. A while later the first young man returned accompanied by a young officer holding handcuffs. Stunned, I was about to laugh, but I gave up the idea at the last moment. He asked for my hand. I gave it to him. The silent young man jumped up and stretched out his hand as well.

"What is wrong?" I asked coolly. Nobody answered. The young officer looked at me doubtfully and started fastening one handcuff round my wrist and the other round the silent young man's wrist. We became tied together. I paid no attention, for I knew that there was nothing I could do. I began to think of my friends who had been detainees over the past years. The problem with these friends was that they were politcally involved in underground activity. What about me? Perhaps some of them were in trouble or, even worse, some had let my name drop for some reason I did not know.

As we left the Police Station and resumed our nowhere journey, the mysterious silence in the car disturbed me. We drove and drove so that I felt it was endless. Finally we came to a halt at a big compound downtown. It was the Ministry of the Interior and also the Headquarters of the Secret Service for National Security. Now, for sure it was for a political reason; of what sort? I did not know!

The first young man walked into a large room followed by the other to whom I was handcuffed. There was a tall handsome man sitting at a fancy desk. As soon as he looked at me he stood up, approached us, and ordered the first young man to release my hand. While my hand was freed he kept looking me over again and again, then put his hand on my shoulders and assumed an expression. Suddenly he fixed his eyes on mine. The other two left.

"Tell me the names of the Saudis you know in Cairo," he said quietly.

The question was not strange. At the time, Cairo was full of Arabs and émigrés from everywhere. There was no difficulty in naming these persons, anyway.

"This third one, Salah, why did you go with him to the University of Cairo last Saturday evening?" asked the tall man.

"I came across him by chance at the outer door of the campus. I had an invitation and was on my way to the main hall to attend Sartre's lecture; that was all," I said.

He turned up his lips, returned to his seat, put on his jacket and came back to me. He looked me over again, held me by the arm and opened the door. Without uttering a word he pulled me very gently, and we walked, arm in arm, through a gloomy corridor.

All the way through my mind hunted for images and incidents to do with that Saudi. What was the trouble? I could not get to any. I felt tired and decided to take everything as it was. Then the tall man stopped before a glass door. He looked through it, and turning more serious he examined me thoroughly, then straightening himself up he took me in. On the door there was a small square sign in brass with only one word written in a beautiful inscription: Director. The room itself was wide and luxuriously furnished; a fat man over fifty with beady piercing eyes was sitting at a big desk. He kept playing with a pen in his hand while looking at me. Silence took over the three of us for a while, then the older man tapped a paper before him, raised his eyes and asked me about my name and job. Once more he asked about the reason why I went to the University. My answer was the same given earlier to the tall man, who stood by me as a teacher in the presence of his headmaster. Though I felt the question was silly the man dismissed my answer with a gesture from his hand and said:

"Liar! You don't know French!" He looked at the other and ordered him to send me to the Castle if I did not speak the truth. With another gesture from his hand he ended the meeting.

Of course you know what happened, my dear; all the same I will repeat it here. Sartre was invited to visit my country. Out of curiousity and being a writer, I had to go, even without knowing any French. The lecture was arranged at the main hall of the University. Because of the bad weather that evening I arrived late. At the outer gate I came across the Saudi who would not stand out in a crowd. In his forties he was still writing clumsy traditional poetry and was fond of literary conversations though his post at the Arab League in Cairo was dealing with oil. His outlook, if conveying anything, conveyed naïveté, especially when it came to politics. The first time I saw him was ten years ago at a Pan-Arab Literary Conference. He was introduced to me as an emigré and our relationship remained superficial all through these ten years. Before seeing him at the entrance of the University more than a year had passed since I last met him. Our meetings always came by chance as you know, either at a common friend's house or at a literary symposium. I knew he was educated at Cairo University and married to an Egyptian. After all he was soft-spoken and 15 years older than I.

That evening, Satre's evening, so to speak, he was accompanied by another man whom he did not introduce. On the way to the door of the hall I saw a young writer with whom I chatted for a while, not introducing him to the Saudi poet and his friend. The four of us were seated in one line on the upper floor, the Saudi to my left, the young writer to my right, and next to him the Saudi's friend. We were not the only ones who came late and missed most of the lecture, but it was something enjoyable to watch an old Frenchman who happened to fascinate the younger generation in the country. Now and then the Saudi would whisper to me about what Satre was saying, but he kept turning over a magazine on his lap. When the lecture was over he got up and we exchanged good-byes. He told me he was leaving the next day for a conference, then went out with his friend. The young writer left separately, but I stayed for a while waiting for the crowd to go; then I struggled through till I got downstairs where I joined a group of writers, who like many others, came to watch.

Dear Truth,

I hope you do not feel bored for I still have a lot to write down.

Back to the tall man's room. I stood up as if in a wilderness, waiting for him to take off his jacket, after which he opened a drawer and took out a hand gun; he put it on the desk and reached for a whip that hung on the wall. Then the first young man entered with a cane. Shortly after him came two others like giants. In a moment a battle erupted from one side; the arms were hands, canes, and a whip; the other side was just there receiving every kind of insult and attack and murmuring or crying. One thing I could catch was your name. They wanted to know you, my dear, but unfortunately you were of no use. During one of the breaks they would have to refresh themselves or to change tactics, I am not sure. The tall man offered me a cigarette and ordered a cup of tea, but made me sit on the floor; then approached me and very gently started to question. I told him all I have mentioned above about the Saudi. He seemed reluctant to believe, but we continued the game of Question and Answer.

"I tell you what this Saudi is; he is a traitor and conspirator," he said.

"Why did you let him go if he was of the kind?" I asked.

"You don't have to question us. You have to answer our questions, truthfully and properly."

"What questions?"

"Why did the two of you go to the University?"

"You'd better ask why I went. That's all I know."

"But he doesn't speak French, does he?"

"I can count more than ten I saw there who don't speak any French or even any language other than Arabic."

"What did he whisper to you while you were sitting?"

"Just comments on the occasion of Sartre's visit."

"Liar! He was telling you other things."

"Why?"

"Because he was whispering, right?"

"Can you speak in a loud voice while you watch a film or listen to a lecture?"

"You Stupid! Don't ask me! I ask you!"

Then the battle would start again. During another break he said:

"Don't try to defend him. We are sure of his situation. We let him go, after we had found out everything."

The words like "traitor" and "conspirator" sounded very strange, but also very cheap, I think. They might be right, they might be wrong, but I am sure I was right about what I told them. I kept wondering to myself: Why not? Might he not be a conspirator or a traitor? Everything was in confusion.

One of the two giants came nearer and said:

"What are his views, I mean politically? What did you hear from him about Egypt and Nasser...such things, you know? If you tell us you will be an eyewitness and no trouble. If you don't you may be sent to the gallows. It is up to you. Think that over anyway and we are waiting. Smoke? Don't you have cigarettes?"

I had cigarettes but they had taken out all the contents of my pockets. The first young man noticed that and handed me my packet, and lit my cigarette. With the first puff I began to realize that my part in this comedy was to contribute something, even against myself. Do you know what happens, my dear, to those who are obsessed by an idea or a problem? They think it over and over, day and night; if someone offers to take all their possessions for giving them the idea or solving the problem in return, they will accept the offer at once. That's what I wished, but all of a sudden, just like turning on a radio, I found it!

The tall man came nearer waving his whip and smiling, and asked:

"How is it going now?"

I looked at him; he nodded, avoiding looking me in the eyes. By then I had decided to play the same game they played. I said:

"Yes, he denounced Nasser once or twice, and used to gossip about our army in Yemen."

They all looked comforted, satisfied; the tall man put his whip on the desk, and said triumphantly:

"Good. And what else?"

The more I went on fabricating such lies in conformity with what they had stated earlier the more happy and content they became. In the end I was rewarded with a cup of tea and a cigarette, but I insisted on smoking mine. Well, lies helped! The tall man ordered a few sheets of paper and asked me to write down all that I told them; he pushed a button and an inside door opened. The first young man took me through and seated me in a smaller adjoining room. Under his guard and another man, I wrote a sort of report, and then the two of them took me downstairs to a completely dark room. Before letting me in they took off my necktie and shoelaces. Overcome by exhaustion I sat down on the floor like the Egyptian Scribe, peeping around in the darkness. I felt the floor with my hand, then blindly I started to feel about the whole room, but I ended up with my hand dirty and nothing in the room except dust. Fully dressed I leaned against a wall and pondered on the "five minutes" and the whole thing. I tried to know the time but my watch was mute and dark. I could not even sleep. The whole cold night passed without my finding any justification for what was happening.

In the early morning the door was opened by an old attendant who bade me good morning, handed me a cup of tea and locked the door. As soon as I swallowed the hot strong tea the door was opened again; this time it was the first young man.

"Come along. Let's go," he said. I hurried along. The same American car was waiting, and we got in. I started to think of shaving and taking a shower at home, but the car turned right and drove in another direction, from which I knew we were going to the old Castle.

While the car was climbing the hill leading to the Castle's gate, the young man asked me to hand him a handkerchief. Innocently enough I handed him the handkerchief, but it turned out against me. With a broad smile on his face, he used it to bind my eyes, and I entered the gate like a blind man. After a short walk inside, full of stumbling along, I heard a harsh voice which invited me to check-in. I found myself verbally filling in a form, like at a hotel, after which I felt a hand dragging me gently by the arm and again I stumbled along, but finally I entered something I could not recognize at first. Then the man took the handkerchief off my eyes, gave it to me and left at once. While he was locking the door from outside, I rubbed my eyes and begun to look about the place. It was a small square cell with two-meter long sides and no windows. Erosion had left its impact together with many inscriptions scattered here and there, as well as some names and dates. The floor was covered with asphalt and looked like a deserted lane full of holes.

Suddenly the door was opened and a stern face looking from over a heap of blankets showed up. He threw the blankets inside and said:

"From this time on your name is four; don't say your own."

The man locked the door and I started looking at the heap and thinking of my new name. A few days later I knew it was the number written with chalk on my black-painted door.

Then the previous night's show started again. I was taken out, eyes bound again, to another place where I heard a voice asking me to take off the bandage. After doing so I found myself in a large room facing two new faces; a gray-haired man sitting at an old desk and resting his chin on a cane in his hand, the other a young plump man standing up by his desk. There were also four or five others. I saw the papers I had written the previous night; they were in front of the old man. He cast a long scrutinizing look at me while his hand was playing with the papers as if weighing them. For a short while, silence prevailed, then he spoke quietly:

"Hey, this isn't enough. We want the truth."

"What truth, sir?"

The man was furious and raised his voice as he said:

"The truth you know and deny; you will be killed if you don't say it."

He stood up and approached me roaring:

"Speak. Tell the truth...otherwise you will see..."

There was nothing to say or do; just the great astonishment which I felt on my face. Two men then moved towards me to handcuff and fetter me. Immediately, I was raised on a bar of iron and suspended from above just like a slaughtered sheep, my head downward, my feet upwards and my body swinging to and fro between two chairs. A third person, tall and stern, began to cane my feet. A few moments later I longed for death. The old man roared:

"How have you met him?"

"By chance..."

"No, you are a liar."

"I am no liar...Ah...Ah...Ah..."

"Bring him down."

I was brought down; all of a sudden the telephone rang. The old man ordered me back to the cell.

The tall stern man came to me there. He looked straight into my eyes and said:

"Be patriotic and speak; respect yourself."

Then he left. What was to be done? The old man had said the meeting at the University hadn't been by chance and this one was doubting my patriotism. It was clear that logic and reason would not do and it was deplorable I had nothing else to help me. My body as you know, my dear, is not strong enough to bear beating. One experience was enough. I went on pacing to and fro along the cell...What had I done previously? Didn't they know me? Wasn't it their job to make investigations before bringing me here? Earlier, at one of the breaks I had confronted them with these questions. The answer was:

"We know you and we know your opinions but you might have erred."

What would happen if they came once more and hung me up? Should I go on lying? I had tried fabrication earlier and it had helped. Why shouldn't I try it another time, if they insisted on hanging up or insulting me? Wasn't this what they wanted? Often, when the sun is shining, nobody cares, but when there's an eclipse, all attention is centered on it. But what was the guilt of this poor man about whom I was fabricating lies? What should I do? What shall I...? What shall...

Again, the door opened. The stern man was right in front of me almost blocking the door with his huge body. He resumed his game of casting doubts on my patriotism. I didn't utter a word. He put his hand in my pocket and brought out the handkerchief to bind my eyes. I was led once more to the Interrogation Office. No more did I care. A state of heedlessness filled me.

(It seems it will be a long letter my dear, I am afraid.)

I only came back to my senses when I found myself hanging in the air. What shall I say? What shall I do? Ah...what...

"Yes, he's a traitor and a conspirator."

The old man roared and the stern man stopped beating me.

"Have you come across him by chance?" he said.

"Yes...Ah...Ah...No. It hasn't been by chance...Yes there has been a date...let me down!" I screamed.

They brought me down and I talked. I fabricated a whole tale, beginning it by admitting the man to be a traitor and a conspirator. I created adequate events and characters. Some of them had no existence and I was careful that the others who were real wouldn't be at hand. I mentioned some known names abroad who could be enemies of the regime. They began to believe the details of the story or that was what I had imagined. For the first time, they ordered tea and cigarettes for me. They looked content and let me sit down. I used all my intelligence, intellect and my experience as a novelist to create a believable story, the hero of which was that man. They asked me about my role in the story. Again I fabricated an adequate role. They started to argue with me. I didn't care and went ahead with my story which came out in the end sound enough. The performance was simply completed and the curtains were drawn. I felt in their faces and smiles a sort of silent applause. They brought me pen and paper to write what was said. Of course, I didn't decline.

All was done so simply, and I returned to my cell in the evening after going to the W.C.

So my dear, I bought my comfort at a cheap price. Talent is sometimes useful. That night, I wasn't able to think much, I swallowed the food they had brought me, then threw myself on the floor with four blankets and made the fifth a pillow under my head. I slept as if I hadn't slept for a month. I don't remember if I had any dreams.

In the morning, the door opened. They brought a light breakfast which I ate. I sat down thinking of the scenario I had drawn up the night before. It seemed it had been terrific and I burst out laughing. But could everything end at this? There were only two alternatives: either to die of beatings and torture or be saved by a miracle. And when the miracle didn't happen, I preferred to escape beatings by using my talent. But this last scenario could easily lead to my death. The least punishment would be execution. For moments, I went on thinking of my destiny. News of the dangerous conspiracy would be published in all newspapers. My photo would be published and I would grow more famous. Correspondents would drown me with their questions and not heed at all my being their former colleague. What would my friends and readers say? I was about to believe that this all would take place. A miracle had to happen.

I spent the whole day thinking of the destiny I had drawn up for myself. All my senses were centered on the door of the cell, waiting for it to be opened at any moment. I couldn't eat any of the food they brought. I was smitten by anxiety. The whole thing was a terrible nightmare. My feet had begun to hurt and I felt them sore and growing so big with pain and inflammation that they filled the cell.

Again, at eight p.m. I had been called to the Interrogation Office which I found busy and crowded like a bus in the rush hour. One of them was the gray-haired man who had interrogated me the day before. They allowed me to sit down before another gray-haired man very much like the former. He asked me solemnly to tell him what happened. He threatened to dissect my body if I hid any detail. Calm and beside myself I went on telling all the details of the scenario I had fabricated the night before. All were listening with great interest. When I reached the end, the man roared:

"You are exaggerating your role; say the truth."

I was about to laugh. I resisted.

"It's what I am saying," I said.

"We have brought the man from the airport. He is here now and he will enter at once...What do you think?"

"Well, I hope he does."

The man looked surprised as he asked:

"Why?"

"To prove to you that he is innocent."

All were stunned. The man scratched his forehead and knocked at the desk with a pen.

"Well...What about the conspiracy?"

"Not true at all."

The man looked more astonished, but he was beside himself as he said:

"Why did you say it?"

"To avoid beating and torture."

All started to look at one another...One laughed. I laughed.

"Then, where's the truth?"

"In the first report I wrote before you brought me here."

The first gray-haired man took the report and went on examining it like someone buying something disagreeable to him.

I didn't know how this last admission had come out. I should have admitted that what I had written was the first gray-haired man's opinions which were in their turn not true at all. I was afraid lest they beat me. I felt some relief for the opinions I had fabricated as the man's were not as dangerous as in the scenario. I was brought back to the cell, hardly believing I had escaped a beating.

(It seems it will be a long letter, my dear, I am afraid.)

I spent such a wretched night. I never closed my eyes...lying had saved me once more.

But couldn't I have held on and stuck to you to the end, dear? No, it is regrettable I am not the type who can bear beatings...or being hurt. I can bear hunger and thirst but not beatings. I longed for death more than once while I was hanging up in the air. Death failed me. How wretched a man can be when he finds no one believing him! Handcuffed...they smote me...I was one and they were many. How could I defend myself? How?

I went on thinking of the coincidence which had led me to this bitter experience.

Wasn't it possible that I could have arrived at the University to attend Sartre's lecture five minutes later or earlier? In Sartre's view Man is born by coincidence and dies by coincidence. Was it the curse of Sartre's existentialism? Suppose arriving later or earlier had actually happened...I wouldn't have been here writing to you now, dear...I would have been free. But the bitter experience imposed itself by choosing me from among the hundreds who had attended the lecture. And perhaps some of them were associates of that riddle of a man whom they didn't let me face. Hasn't Man invented devices to detect lying without resorting to beatings? Beating is the oldest means ever known for torture and punishment. It is deplorable, however, that it is still used despite the great scientific progress of the age. I can justify beating sometimes as a way of punishing or imposing discipline. But in my case I can't find any justification. Why has it been impossible for you to appear without resorting to such a thing as beating? Isn't it the job of these people to detect and find you out without resorting to violence? I can't find any justification for what they have done to me except that they were hiding their disability. They have the potential to know the time I take my meal, the time I go to the W.C. and even what's going on between a man and his wife in their bedroom. However, they have ignored what science and progress have offered them and resorted to the oldest way known by mankind to detect and discover you.

I couldn't make out why I remembered Galileo on that night. He was brought to stand trial before the Inquisition for his freethinking and infidelity. The punishment was known. Many scientists had been executed earlier. What did Galileo do? He must have found himself in the same position as mine. If he admitted you simply, this would end in his death. But, if he denied you, he would gain life. And because Galileo loved life, he denied you.

I used to condemn Galileo and deplore his cowardice. Now, however, I have come to respect him and find excuses for his stand. Socrates was brave up to death, while Galileo was coward up to life. Galileo was an aged man. I am young and naturally I am interested in life. But this wasn't the reason I lied. The main reason was to avoid being hit and therefore I denied you, dear, when they whipped me. Socrates drank poison and died. But our time isn't that of Socrates. Don't think, dear, that I am trying to justify my cowardice when I have denied you.

That night I felt the cell expanded to contain almost all my past, my reading and my relations. I learned one lesson: freedom is the only thing from which you yourself are inseparable.

In that cell I spent about two months. I never slept during the first ten days. Only when I got used to sounds of human pain, screams and sighs that reached me from nearby cells, was I able to sleep. Many times I longed for death so that I would not hear the painful orchestra of the place. Every time I heard feet approaching my door I would hurry to put on my socks as I thought they would protect me when caned. Whenever the door of the cell opened I would search for my handkerchief. I kept wondering: what would I say to my people and friends? They knew that I was an advocate of the regime. Such an experience, no doubt, would have its impact on one's life and relations. I thought of committing suicide, but there was no available means; they had taken everything except my watch which I put in my pocket.

During that time the old gray-haired man used to bring me to his room to make sure of the reality of the Scenario. He once confided to me that his job was to doubt 90% of what people, like myself, say. Another time I argued that, in law, one is innocent until proven guilty. He laughed and said:

"That's in law only!" When he got tired of arguing he would dismiss it by saying I was philosophizing!

One day in the afternoon my door was opened. A young man smiled at me and said:

"Put on your clothes and be ready to go."

I believed him and I got ready in minutes. He came back a while later and shouted:

"Come along!"

I went out of the cell. The daylight dazzled my eyes for a while. In the hall was a queue of more than twenty people that I was told to join. I recognized six of them, but no word was permitted. Then we were told to leave the Castle one by one. A big black van was waiting for us. When the van moved everybody felt relief and we started to talk to each other. We were all there for the same reason: either friends of relatives of the Saudi. Some of us had never seen him, but were friends of friends. To my surprise I found the young writer whom I met that evening and who did not speak to the Saudi! Two of us were over sixty; another two were an old man and his son; a strange combination of ages, professions and beliefs, but most of us were writers and poets. Seeing the van turning to Torah, where we are now being kept, one screamed:

"No use!"

From what I learned later some of them had resorted to lies just as I did in order to avoid beatings, and ten of them, myself included, were sacked. Most important of all was that we discovered, from some relations of the Saudi, that he was still free and safe!

It was a long letter, my dear. This is enough for the moment. For if I let my pen write it will go on and on. If I were free I would tell you all about this camp where I stay, together with more than two thousand detainees. I might write to you again, anyway.

Only there is something trivial enough I have forgotten to tell you about. Can you believe that I have lost any desire to get out of this place after I have seen and heard what is here; not out of despair or pessimism, but out of a wish to enjoy a limited and defined experience inside here unlike the unlimited and undefined one outside.

I have forgotten to tell you, as well, that the two thousand inmates came over some years ago, and I found out after listening to their stories that what has been done with me is far less than what has happened to them.

Dear Truth,

I hope my story did not bore you, and waiting for a word from you will you accept my love and hope that you remain alive and free.

Yours ever,
S. Hamza

P.S.

Sender of this open letter discovered that he, under certain circumstances, has lost the address of his beloved Truth. Anyone who finds it is kindly requested to send this letter onto her.

May God reward the finder along with thanks of the sender.

Born in 1935, Ali Shalash earned his M.A. at Cairo University. He is a writer, literary critic, lecturer and journalist who is fluent in Arabic, English and French. His contributions include short stories, essays, translations, talks and interviews in various newspapers, literary magazines, and radio throughout Arab countries, England and the USA.

"I certainly won't trouble her,
but she does make me curious."

The Tide Woman

BY FRØYDIS PETERSEN

THEY say she is crazy. Perhaps she is. I've sat and looked at her each evening for an entire month now. She has probably gotten used to me sitting there. I'm probably a little crazy myself—in any case, outcast and unsuccessful. I've given up my middle-class life. Somewhere else in this country sits a woman who feels glad to be free of me. A household goes on without me. Two teenagers perhaps think about me, but care about me most when I'm away. A dog would wag its tail if I came, but I've lost my right to that door.

Klausen is a friendly man. He doesn't say much. I help him with his small fields that are spread out among the knolls. I cultivate strawberry fields and thin out carrots. Between those jobs we dig up stones and lay them out in long rows in places where nothing can grow anyway.

I help Klausen, and he helps me. I get room and board and money, most of which is sent directly to that other place in this country. Not enough money for me to be able to go to the city and buy myself a bottle. And that isn't the idea anyway. I go to the store, buy myself tobacco and one newspaper or another. In the evenings I sit here in the hollow of a sloping rock by the sea. On a clear evening I can see a mass of reefs and skerries. There's usually a light wind blowing, a gentle breeze over the hollow. There's always the sound of the breakers on the sand, the gurgle and splash of water against rock and seaweed. There's the screaming of gulls, and often the buzz of motorboats. During the day the rocks and the small beach below may be covered with towels, beach bags, plastic toys and the other paraphenalia that visitors to the beach need to have with them. I don't see that. I never come during the day. I come after the last bather has left. Then the beach is mine.

And hers. The old woman's. I have christened her the Tide Woman. True, the name isn't original with me. It came from the Swedish singer Alf Hambe. He sings about the Tide Woman in his driftwood song: "The Tide Woman bends and rinses in the sea, washing away islands and scum, sweeping..."

The Tide Woman *here* also sweeps. And she too waits until the last bather has gone. A long dark skirt covers her feet. I think she is barefoot, but I can't know for certain. She has a shawl over her shoulders. It hangs down in points, one in front and one in back. A poncho, I guess it's called. On her head she wears a kerchief. She has pulled it so far forward that I can't see her face. In her hand is a broom. If I didn't know better, I might have thought she was about to ride off for a witches' coven. But witches surely don't exist?

She always begins at the top of the smooth, sloping rock. Sweeps bread crumbs, bottle caps, ice cream wrappers and other trash downward. Uses her whole body. She works steadily, without giving me a single glance. When she is finished, she collects all the garbage and places it alongside the overflowing trash can. Then she sweeps the beach with light, quick strokes. She bends down and picks up plastic wrappers, empty bottles, tubes and cardboard containers. Carries it all to the trash can. Goes back and searches the sand. Finally she sweeps seaweed and shells out into the sea. A dark stripe forms on the edge of her skirt after a while. She doesn't mind that it gets wet.

I ask Klausen about her. "She's a little crazy," he answers. "She lives alone in the small captain's cottage on the point. She's a little crazy, yes," he says again, probably knowing more than he will let on. "But she's not dangerous. She came here eight, nine years ago. The house had been empty a long time. She never says anything, and we leave her alone. Once in a while she shops at the store. But she only gets ads and bills in the mail, and she never has visitors. Most likely she inherited the captain's cottage. Poor old thing, she probably has her reasons. And we leave her alone."

He looks at me as he says the last words. And I understand his meaning. I certainly won't trouble her, but she does make me curious.

I go to the shore in all kinds of weather. The Tide Woman comes also. When it's foggy, I sense her only as a slightly darker part of the air. Between the howls of the foghorn I hear her broom scrape against stone.

One evening there is a fresh breeze and rain. No one has been there during the day. The wind has arrived ahead of the Tide Woman. It sweeps and polishes so there is nothing more for a lone broom to do. Nevertheless, she comes at the same time. Her skirt balloons around her, presses together, streams out behind her, bulges and flaps about her. She stands with her broom, lets the wind tear at her clothing and looks out over the waves. Soon her clothes are soaking wet and heavy. They hang straight down. Then she puts down her broom and raises her arms in the air. She turns her face upward. It shines whitely. Her shawl pastes itself about her head. Then she dances a strange slow dance on the sand. She bends this way and that. Glides slowly around, glides along the water's edge. Lifts her arms in an arc over her head and laughs. I can hear her laugh. The wind brings snatches of her laughter. I am no more present for her than the stones beside me. She doesn't see us. Doesn't care to see.

One day I chance to pass her cottage. In the doorway sits a cat. It is orange and white. It is an affectionate cat, because as soon as it sees me it gets up, raises its tail and comes toward me; purring, it rubs itself against my legs. I bend down and pet it. It walks past me, stretches, comes back, and is very happy to be stroked. It is clean and delicate. The fur is smooth and shiny.

So she is not completely alone. She has someone who needs milk and food. I squat down and talk to the car. There are climbing roses along the wall here, but other than that no garden—only "nature." A few bumblebees buzz to and fro, and the terns scream here just as everywhere else in this part of the country. The cottage is white like all the other houses in this community. It could use a paint job, I notice. There is also an outbuilding, a shed. I hear someone chopping, and there stands the Tide Woman with rolled-up sleeves. She has already chopped a small pile of wood.

"Good day," I say. She doesn't look up, doesn't allow herself to notice that there is anyone else present. She picks up an armful of the newly-chopped wood and carries it into the shed. Meanwhile I borrow the ax and begin chopping. She comes back, picks up another armful of wood. She wears only a blouse over the skirt today. She doesn't acknowledge my presence, and I can't chop fast enough. When she has carried in all the wood that's been cut, she goes into the cottage and closes the door after herself. I chop a large pile and carry it into the shed for her. I continue the pattern of logs she has started there. Looking around I see that everything is orderly and well-cared-for. For someone who's crazy, she's astonishingly practical. Tools and equipment hang on the wall. A pair of oars stand upright in the corner. Fishing nets hang over a beam. I won't poke around in other people's things.

In the evening she comes to the beach as usual. There is much to sweep. She doesn't see me.

The next time I pass her cottage, she has begun to paint it. She's standing on a stepladder. Over her skirt she wears a transparent plastic apron.

"Good day," I say, but she doesn't hear. She paints with long strokes. I go into her shed. There I will find what I'm looking for—another brush. I only want to help, but when I begin to paint she carefully climbs down the ladder. She goes inside and closes the door as before. Her cat sits in the window and looks at me. I paint the entire wall, come again the next day and continue. She hasn't painted any more in the meantime. I paint her entire house. It is done in a few afternoons. I don't expect any thanks, and don't get any either. I haven't thought about whiskey for several days.

Klausen tells me he can use me in the winter too. He intends to pull down walls inside his old house. Then he wants to modernize it and rent it out to summer guests. I'm to have that job he says. I can take as much time as I need. His wife nods in agreement, and his children absolutely want me to stay. So I stay. And in fact I'm happy too.

It is now too cold to sit on the rocks. No one leaves trash on them any longer either. And no one comes and sweeps them. Once in a while I go past the Tide Woman's cottage. Often I find something to do for her, but usually I have to decide on it myself. If she is doing something and I try to give her a hand, she only stops doing it and goes inside and closes the door.

"Good day," I say each time we meet, and that is all that is said between us. Now that I've seen her up close I realize she isn't as old as I thought. She is quite thin. Probably doesn't eat much.

Strange that it snows so much so far south in this country. I've shoveled paths between the buildings at Klausen's. His children jump from the second story. It looks like such fun that I try it too. The children love it. Grownups don't often play here. Nor other places, for that matter. I think about the Tide Woman and the path to her house. The highway has been plowed, but her house lies far back from the road. I borrow the shovel and spade from Klausen. He says he'll come along and help me. It takes us several hours to shovel our way from the road to her house. The path between her house and the shed she has managed to clear herself. Klausen returns home, but I clear off the roof of the shed. Tomorrow I'll come back and do the roof of her cottage. I wonder how she has managed in previous winters.

Liv Fjell is her name. I ask Klausen if he knows her name. "Liv Fjell," he replies. Not Mrs. or Miss. I don't have any right to use the name, but then I don't really have the right to call her Tide Woman either. She isn't a caricature, but a person who sweeps her beach and clears her plot of land. I believe I've heard her name before. Liv Fjell. I've heard someone say it, but I haven't connected it with her. I clear the path to her place after each snowfall. Occasionally I meet her and come out with my inevitable "Good day." I don't need to. I don't know if she has good days. Or bad ones, for that matter.

For two weeks I've been bar-hopping in the city. Klausen, good person that he is, hunted me down and brought me back. His children stand in the doorway staring at me. Afterwards I see myself in the mirror. I'm unshaven and hungover. My eyes are sunken far back in my head. Mrs. Klausen comes with a washbasin. Then she leaves and after a while she returns with a bowl of hot soup. She asks me to eat slowly, is full of concern and doesn't say a word of reproach.

One day I'm making a fire in the wood stove. My eyes fall on something in an old city newspaper behind the woodbin. It's an announcement of a ballet: "Liv Fjell dances *Sleeping Beauty.*" Yes, I've heard the name before.

Spring demands something from a man, here as other places. Perhaps more here. The stones grow first. No one has planted them, but they rise from the ground nevertheless. Klausen says there are just as many stones every spring. We pick up stones, roll stones, make piles of stones. First one's hands get blisters that break and burn, then one gets tough, hard skin. Klausen has his calluses from last year and the year before. I'm not able to pick up as many as he, but I still do a decent day's work.

Liv Fjell has cleared the stones from her little garden plot before I'm able to help her, so instead I get a hoe and turn over the earth for her. She sows carrots, peas and radishes, sets out potato eyes, and plants cabbage and cauliflower. At the back of the house she has a little homemade greenhouse, a few old windowpanes set at a slant. One day I see tomato plants behind the glass. Rhubarb pushes its way to the light. Scallions appear. Liv has sown parsley and lettuce. Yes, this is going to be a self-sufficient homestead. I want to surprise her; I turn new land near the wall and sow peppers and cucumbers. The cat has a heavy belly and lazily oversees that I do a good job. Then one day I no longer see her. I realize that she is busy inside with a litter of kittens.

The sloping rocks of the beach beckon. I find the old hollow from last year, and sit there and philosophize. Thoughts stream through me, become entwined in each other, slip away. There is something I want to catch hold of, but can't find. It's something I should have thought. I know the thought is hiding just around the corner—the explanation to why I went off the track like a strange train.

Liv Fjell comes in her long skirt. She doesn't have her broom along. She walks along the beach, searching. Then she bends down and takes hold of a piece of driftwood. It is nearly black, slippery and heavy. She drags it up on the sand. It leaves a long track. The waves lick it and erase the track as far as the water reaches. Liv isn't able to lift the log by herself. I go down and lift with her. She drops her end. I do the same. She continues to stand there. Then picks up the log again. So do I, and we carry it, one at each end, over the rocks to her house. There we lay it down by the chopping block. Liv is silent as always. She turns and goes back to the beach. I follow her. She doesn't find any more logs, but she finds crooked branches which she picks up, turns over and examines, then throws down again. She takes one branch with her. I let her go.

Now I go to the beach every evening. Liv comes too. She picks up stones and shells, puts them in a large basket. In bad weather she dances. Sometimes she holds her arms straight out from her body and dances round and round, now and then bowing graciously toward the sea.

I get a letter from the woman I had to leave. She has found work and doesn't want any more money, except for child support. That's good of her. I have a bit more for myself, but I don't go to the city. I buy lumber at the store. Then I do carpentry work in Liv's shed. I also set up a little plot enclosed by chicken wire. Liv doesn't say anything, and perhaps I shouldn't make things at other people's places on my own like that. Then I buy two hens. One day one of them lays a beautiful, white egg. I pick it up in my hand and go to Liv with it. No one answers when I knock. Then, without being invited, I open the door and go in. I come into a kitchen. There are flowers on the windowsill and braided rugs on the floor. The cat lies in a basket, licking her young. Liv sits at the table drinking coffee. She doesn't look up.

"Good day," I say as usual. "Here is the first egg from your hens."

Now Liv looks at me. She has large, beautiful eyes. She pushes the coffee cup away from her and says:

"Please sit down."

Frøydis Petersen lives quietly in Norway earning her living as an English teacher. Dorrit Berg translated the story which is an excerpt from Miss Petersen's novel Vrakgods.

"The past could also be a prison, Father."

Waywaya

BY F. SIONIL JOSÉ

THE first time Dayaw crossed the river, he felt fulfilled, as if he had finally passed the greatest test of all. It was so unlike that leap over the flaming pit—the feat of strength that would have assured his father, the Ulo, that he was no weakling, that in spite of his seeming indolence and love of poetry and singing, he was capable nonetheless of courage as were the bravest warriors of Daya. All his life he had been cooped up like the pigs his mother fattened in the pit before they were taken out for the feasts. Daya, after all, was hemmed in to the east by the sea, vast and mysterious, and to the west, this mighty river, for beyond it was forest and mountain, land of the Taga Laud, the ancient and indomitable enemy of his people.

He had made the crossing at night after he had blackened his face and body with soot, carrying with him nothing but a coil of *maguey* twine and his long knife; he had dashed from the cover of reeds near the river's bank, for while Apo Bulan showed the way, it would also reveal him to whoever watched the river.

Days afterwards, he tried to fathom the reasons for the deed, why he went alone, and for what. For one—the river was there, a barrier to knowledge of new things, new sights, and perhaps a new life. He was, indeed, aglow with wanting to know; how many times had he mused, gazing at the changing cloud patterns in the sky, the shapes of the waves as they broke and foamed on the beach, the track of ants, the wheeling of birds—they all seemed to follow a design that could not be unraveled, just as one could not know what lay beyond the river and the sea without crossing them.

Once he climbed the lofty *dalipawen* at the edge of the communal farms and as if he was on some promontory, he scanned the world around him—the shining sea in the east and beyond the green, mangly top of the forest, far down the horizon to the west, the mountains, purplish green in the last light of day. He envied those who lived there for they could see everything. Was it possible for them to know everything as well?

Wading across the river in the dry season was not difficult; there were islands of reeds and upturned trees dragged down from the mountains with their catch of moss or dried leaves, and clear pools where there would be silverfish and shells. This was how it felt then, to ford this limit of what was safe. From the very beginning, it was dinned to him, and to all the young Taga Daya—to cross the river meant going to war.

The first time he came to this river was when he was thirteen and was with some twenty boys of the same age; they had marched for one day and one night, in anxiety and fear, for they had no warriors to protect them but this old, shriveled healer who made this journey every year. They had been taught stealth and cunning, and once they entered the forest beyond the cultivated fields and *cogon* wastes, it was possible for the enemy to be lurking there. They were not warriors—they would be hogtied and brought to Laud as slaves. For a day, they walked without eating and by the morning of the next day, when they finally reached the river, they were weak, hungry and ready to die. Only the fear of capture kept them alive. There, on the sandy bank, behind the tall reeds that had flowered with plumes of dazzling white, they lined up, squatting while the healer sharpened his knife and prepared the strange mixture of tobacco and weeds with which he treated their wounds after he had circumcised them.

He was now on his third night and the relentless sense of danger that hounded him was no longer as keen as it had been on the first, particularly when a dog had howled and a man had come out with a lighted pine splinter and a spear, wondering perhaps what lizard was out there after his chickens. He had slithered into the recesses of the bush and returned afterwards. He knew the town by then, and in the waning moonlight, he stole away from it, detoured through the terraces in the mountainside, then down to the forest of scrub and *cogon*, making a new way each time. It was still dark when he reached the river. He had already satisfied most of his curiosities; he had seen the young play in the moonlight, heard their songs, their conversations. He had looked at their handiwork, their fields of sweet potato and rice, and marveled at the quality of their crafts.

He returned to the cove—actually a small turn of the river that was hidden by a wall of low branches. Within it was a pool that was fed by a spring and beyond the spring, up a sandy bar, was a sprout of *cogon* behind which he had slept the night before. He had taken care that there was no trace of him in the sand so that when he went to the spring to drink, he had wiped his tracks carefully. Now he went to sleep, and once rested, he would merely race across the river to the sanctuary of his own land.

It was long past morning when he woke up, alive to the twitter of birds, the jabber of monkeys, the scent of moss and green living things. He lay on his back motionless for some time, gazing at the cloud-flecked sky. It was then that a rustling to his right jarred him from his reverie; he keened to the footfalls on the grass and dried leaves. Whoever was approaching was not trying to hide his presence.

Then she burst into view, a girl lovely as morning and just as fair, her hair knotted to the left above her ear. A fine, blue tattoo of flower designs ran in a thin line down her arms to her wrists. She knelt down before the rim of the pool and gazed at her reflection there, then stood up, untied the knot of her blue sack dress on her shoulder let it slip down to her feet. She stood—naked and true and beautiful, her face upraised to catch a bit of sun, her breasts and nipples touched with pink. Her stomach was flat and below the patch of pubic hair, her legs were supple and well shaped; she stooped and untied the thongs ot her leather sandals then she walked nimbly into the water, shivering at first as she tested it with her toe. Then she plunged and splashed about. She dived to the shallow depths and in the clear water, he could follow her lissome figure turning, then surfacing to float on her back, so that her breasts were shiny with water and sun.

Dayaw watched, keeping his ears keen; he wanted to know if she had companions but he could hear only the rustle of the wind in the trees, the gurgling of the river as it coursed through boulders and shallows. He had stashed across the river an iron plowshare, a piece of newly woven cloth, a quiver of iron-tipped arrows. Now, he would also bring home a slave—healthy, young and good to look at. With her sandals, her bangles of gold, she was no simple peasant; she must come from the upper class of Laud. His agile mind quickly devised a way by which he could capture her with the least resistance and trouble.

It seemed that she would swim forever but finally, she made for her clothes. By then, Dayaw had crouched closer to her things and as she stooped to gather them, he rushed out and pinned her arms, clamping a hand over her mouth. That was a mistake for she bit his hand; the pain was sharp and his response was immediate. He spun her around and struck her in the jaw. There was this dumb, surprised look on her face as she staggered backwards and fell. Dayaw bound her hands and feet, and gagged her mouth. He gathered her clothes, her sandals, then erased the signs ot struggle on the sand. And heaving her on his shoulders, he headed for the river.

It did not matter very much that he would cross now in the daylight; if they pursued him, he could easily outrace them, and once he was in the sanctuary of his forest, it was a brave man who would follow him. Once or twice, while he was knee-deep in water, he turned to look, and again when he was finally across. No one had seen him.

Once across, he laid her on the grass, still naked, while he went back to the water to wash the soot of three days from his face and body. When he returned, she had revived and she cringed at his approach.

"You are heavy!" Dayaw said, smiling. "And look at my hand—you little wildcat!"

He waved his right hand which had begun to swell, her teeth marks deeply imprinted still below the thumb. She made angry protesting sounds, shaking her head. She tried to rise but when she realized it was useless to struggle she did not move anymore. In the sunlight, looking closer at her, she seemed fairer and prettier than when he first saw her. That was what the Taga Laud women were noted for, unlike the women of Daya, who had darker skin.

"You are good for the eyes," Dayaw said, moving closer and tweaking her nipples. She glared at him but did not move and very soon the nipples hardened. Pleased with himself, Dayaw smiled. "If you promise not to make trouble," he said with a laugh, "I will give you back your clothes."

She nodded quickly.

"We have a long way to go—a whole day's march, and I don't want to carry you." He helped her to her feet and as she stood up, he realized that she was tiny, she did not even reach up to his shoulder. He went beside her and ran a hand down the curve of her back to her buttocks. Then he untied her hands and feet. Free at last, she stretched her arms and stamped her feet. She picked the sack dress up and put it on. When she looked at him again, entreaty was in her eyes.

"Yes, I will hit you again," he said, raising his fist, "if you cannot be tamed. And I don't want to do that."

Shortly before midday, he found the water tubes, the dried meat and the cakes of brown sugar that he had hidden under the trunk of a dead tree. He ate ravenously and when he was through, he gave her a little of what was left. She was hungry, and thirsty, too, but she refused what he offered her.

Dayaw shrugged. "If you don't want to eat, then march on an empty stomach."

By nightfall, she still had not spoken a word. Her jaw had begun to swell and he wondered if he had hit her so hard that her tongue had been cut. In the dimming light, he held her face. She winced. "Open your mouth," he said, but she refused. He glared at her and raised his fist. Slowly, she opened her mouth. No, her tongue was not cut and her breath was warm and sweet like a baby's upon his face.

He gazed at the sullen eyes, at the mouth, the nose; yes, he really had a good-looking slave, perhaps better looking than any of the young women he knew, even Liwliwa with whom he already spent many nights.

They reached a gulley where saplings grew and at this time of the year, the gulley was dry. He told her to recline against a sapling. He tied her hands behind the young tree and then her feet. It was not that he feared treachery; it was that she might run away and be captured by another Taga Dava and he would then lose all claim to her. She seemed resigned and not once did she protest.

The dark came quickly. Fireflies emerged from the tall grass and winked at them. The stars were out; it would be some time before the rains came. He was tired but sleep was slow in coming. He turned on his side. She was leaning against the tree, her legs raised. In the soft dark, he could see the outline of her face in quiet repose.

"What is your name?"

She did not answer.

"I am Dayaw," he said, "the older son of the Ulo. My younger brother, Parbangon, will be circumcised before the rains start. Do you know any Laud songs?"

No reply.

"I like to sing. I make my own songs. Listen—he quickly formed the lines and gave a tune to them:

> "The river is deep
> But we can ford it.
> Who will make the bridge?
> Perhaps love will do it.
> Perhaps time will prove it..."

He paused. "Do you like it?"

The pensive face was immobile, the eyes closed as if in thought.

"You don't like music," he said. "You silly girl. Going there alone and so far away from home. What were you doing there by yourself, anyway?" He paused and laughed, "Well, you may just as well ask what I was doing there, too."

Silence again, the soughing of the wind in the grass, crickets alive in the bushes. "It was Apo Langit that brought me there, that brought you there. It was Apo Langit that made you my slave..." For an instant he wanted to untie her and have her submit to him but he vanquished the thought; he was not going to use force, she should go to him because she wanted to the way Liwliwa wanted him. And it was Liwliwa and her promise of welcome that was in his thoughts when sleep finally claimed him.

In the morning, he was rudely wakened and when he opened his eyes, he realized that she had kicked him, not in anger but because she was in pain. She had slipped, twisted her back and could not rise. He stood up and looked at her wrists; they were swollen. He was determined to teach her obedience, to humble her, but the pain in her face touched him and he untied the twine that bound her wrists. She quickly withdrew her hands from behind her. He untied her legs next and free at last, she stood up and limped to the bushes down the gulley. He did not go after her—she was just going to urinate but when she did not return, he followed her.

She was lying on her stomach on the grass and crying silently. Then she turned to him. "Why don't you kill me and let me suffer no more?"

It was the first time that she had spoken and he understood everything; but for the different intonation, she was speaking in his own tongue.

"You are in our land now," he said coldly. "You are a captive, a slave and you will be killed, of course, if you try to run away. You know that. Your life is in your hands." Then, abruptly, as a warrior would speak: "Let us go."

She stood up and followed him quickly.

Before noon, they reached the fringes of Daya, the well-groomed fields that were being prepared for the seed. His first impulse was to do what was customary, to strip her, parade her through the town and humiliate her. The swelling of her jaw had subsided and in its place was a dark bruise. Her wrists had bled when the twine was cut. But he did not undress her; he merely tied her wrists again, this time loosely, and then marched with her in tow. Thinking about it later, he was to realize why he did not want her naked. He had seen her in her glory; he coveted her and did not want others to see her as he had seen her then.

Out of their houses, where they were cooking the noon day meal, came the women, the children, and the menfolk who were not working in the fields or at the beach. The children gathered around her, fingering her dress, touching her bangles and jeering at her. Her head erect, she looked straight ahead as she walked but her eyes were frightened and once or twice she stumbled.

"Dayaw, that is some trophy!"

"Can she cook?"

"Can she weave?"

"Can she gyrate her hips?"

"Is she juicy and tight?"

They shrieked and laughed and Dayaw laughed with them, acknowledging their greetings, pleased that they knew where he had been, proud that they could see his slave and also the new quiver, the piece of cloth slung on his shoulder and the plowshare under his arm.

He let the day lengthen, though courtesy demanded that he should have gone straight to the Ulo, his father, to tell him that he was back. He had not told anyone where he was going, not even Parbangon who often came to his house to listen to his songs and his *kutibeng*.

Liwliwa came shortly after noon with a bowl of eggplants and bitter melons cooked with tomatoes, onions and dried fish, and a pot of rice. Her hair was glossy with coconut oil, and while he reclined after they had eaten, she kneaded his muscles with oil and stirred him; while the slave girl washed pots outside, she closed the bamboo door and welcomed him in the way he had expected it.

When he woke up, Liwliwa had gone and his slave was in the room, fanning him with a small palm leaf. He showed her where she should sleep, a corner of the kitchen, among the fish traps and cooking pots, and told her what her chores would be, from sunup to sundown. She listened intently. Women passed and peeped, and children who had not seen her earlier shouted obscenities at her.

"Now, what shall I call you?" he asked, as he made ready to visit the Ulo.

"Waywaya," she said, bowing. He could see that she was crying again and he hated the sight of women in tears.

At this time of day, the Ulo would be in the community house, acting out his duties, dispensing advice and help to those who needed it, allocating rice seed for the next planting season as well as the new plots to be cleared and new duties. Dayaw loved his father and had not meant to appear disobedient, but through the years, his interests had veered; while the other youths would listen to the talk of the elders, he got bored and would go by himself to the forest or to the beach. He was no weakling, but while the other youths practiced the arts of war and exercised for the great leap that would transform them into men, he played with his *kutibeng* and took pleasure in composing new songs. When the great feast came, he was not even anxious. They had lighted the wide pit and the hay and logs there were a roaring flame. They lined up—the young men who would now be warriors, and one by one, they leaped across the chasm of fire. They had practiced and he had not and when it was his turn, he started to panic for he now realized that the pit was wider than he thought it would be. He ran and leaped just the same and barely made it to the other side; he had burned his foot—the stigma that his father would bear—but he thought nothing of it. The final test, after all, was when the warrior crossed the river.

He had done that, been in Laud for three nights, and what did he learn? Were the warriors of Laud all that skilled and ferocious? Were they out to destroy Daya and everything his father and his people had built?

This was what his father had told him and all Taga Daya; he had heard this when he was small, and again when he trained and he still heard it now that the Ulo had begun to age and a few strands of white laced his mane. Still, he was the Ulo, the repository of wisdom and strength until that time when someone braver, stronger and wiser would lead them to battle.

The community house came into view—a magnificent structure as tall as a bamboo, with a high-pitched roof that was almost an arm's length in thickness, so thick that it could last a hundred years! The flooring was solid *parunapin,* taken from the forest and drawn across the gulleys by water buffaloes. The bamboo on the walls had been tempered in brine so that all the insects would not be able to attack it. The posts—almost as fat as a man's thigh, were the best *sagat* there was. And above the walls, just below the eaves were the skulls of their enemies, impaled on ratton staves.

He waited until everyone had gone, then the Ulo beckoned to him. His dark, handsome face was shrouded in gloom. "Do you know that had you not returned today, tomorrow we would have dispatched men to Laud to look for you?"

"Forgive me, Father," Dayaw said contritely.

"Well, how far did you go?"

"I crossed the river, Father." He wanted to say more but he held back.

"And what else did you do?"

"I wanted to know the enemy..."

"That is a foolish thing to do, going there alone, with no one behind you. And this girl..."

Dayaw smiled. "She is a wildcat but I can tame her. I will know more about Laud from her. But this I already know—the Taga Laud—they are like us and I think they want peace."

"So do we," the Ulo said. "But time has a momentum and we must be ready for war. Always. And you don't prepare for war by reciting poetry and going on an adventure by yourself..."

Again, the sarcasm. The Ulo did not hide it anymore, his frustration that his older son, bright with tunes and words and wise in his own way—did not have any feeling for combat, for politics, for the craft of ruling. He was getting on in years and to whom would he pass this accumulated wisdom and experience? Dayaw, his son, his blood, but he had been claimed by the talisman of forest and sea when it was all before him, the opportunity to rule, to unite, conquer not just Laud but also the many regions beyond Daya, the lands of Abagatan and Amianan.

When Dayaw was still young he had looked upon the Ulo with awe; it had pleased him to know that his father was a leader, respected and loved, that it was he who led the warriors and had given Taga Daya a sense of unity—their best defense against their enemies—which had eluded them for years. With the years, however, he had also seen the panoply of power and of ceremony that had consumed the Ulo, that for all his avowals of justice, he was not beyond the reach of fawning relatives and panderers. He could not understand how in a year of drought his mother could still go down the far reach of Amianan bringing with her a retinue of friends, honey and rice in two boatloads, and return with nothing but beads and gushing talk about lavish feasts given by the rich and powerful whom she had met.

He could not understand how his mother's brother could continue in blessed idleness while everyone worked, how his father could hand over grain from the communal granary to his favorite warriors who had not even fought in Laud. There were times when the people grumbled and had less to eat—but the Ulo had brought them peace, the right to work and live without the Taga Laud descending from the mountain to badger their lives.

"The war must stop, Father," he said quietly.

"And you took a slave," the Ulo hissed at him. "This means that they will seek revenge."

His father was right and again, he was clobbered not by superior intelligence but by his own impulsiveness. If he had only carefully thought out the consequences of the deed. And thinking about it later, he recognized this magic compulsion about Waywaya that he could not exorcise. Again, it came to him not as a flash of lightning, but just as searing, the knowledge that his perdition was in himself. He went down the wooden stairs into the wide grassy yard and once more, the urge to leave Daya came. How often had he thought about it but always, he seemed rooted in the land. When the ships of the Narrow Eyes docked at the stone pier which they had built from coral, he had often wondered if they could take him so that the niggling doubts, the nagging sentiments would be banished forever. However, after the Narrow Eyes had loaded the tobacco and the rice in exchange for knives, plates and beads, they would leave and he would not even tarry to ask that they take him.

It was dusk when he reached his house and from the distance he saw Parbangon idling at the foot of the stairs, strumming the *kutibeng*. His younger brother would probably be with him the whole night, asking a host of questions, listening to his new songs.

Waywaya kept house. Liwliwa sneered at her and envied her for she was doing what she, herself, would have wanted to do had Dayaw but asked her. She said Waywaya would not be able to last; her ways, her attitudes were different and all because she was from Laud. The older women made the same remarks—she was alien to the ways of Daya. But in time, all the pots in the kitchen were clean of soot, the firewood rack below the house was neatly stacked and there was always husked grain in the bin. The grass roof was patched where it had thinned and where the rattan twine on the floor had loosened, she had tightened it so that the split bamboo was once more taunt and secure.

Waywaya asked if she could weave and Dayaw retrieved one of the old looms his grandmother had left, and there was enough cotton too and vegetable dyes which she mixed in a way different from the women of Daya. She did not use the patterns from where she came; she fashioned new ones, using the primary reds and blacks of the Taga Daya and in time, she made trousers for Dayaw, for Parabangon and last of all, a dress for herself.

There were many nights that Dayaw did not sleep in his house, he loitered often in the communal house for the unmarried, and when the weather was good, he would go to the beach or the fields with Liwliwa. And when he returned in the morning, there was the usual plate of steaming rice, the bowl of ginger broth which she had brewed, the perfunctory questions about how the night had been, if he slept well, and inevitably, how Liwliwa was.

Once, he woke up in the night with a parched throat and he went to the water jar for a drink. She was awake and sat up. In the dark, he went to her and for a moment he wanted to touch her. There was no stopping him; she was his property, but he remembered the past impulsiveness that had been damnation and he withdrew, hissing to himself: *Lightning! Lightning!*

It was good year; the rice grew tall, Apo Langit had been kind and the harvest was abundant. By the time the easterly winds began to blow, the fields had all been gleaned, the bat wing ships of the Narrow Eyes were rounding the point again; they brought more jars and plates, more bells and gongs. The slaves were even given new clothes, some were set free, but they elected to remain to partake of Daya's peace and prosperity.

A good year, but not for Waywaya. She had her first horrible bout with fever before the harvest and though Parbangon came and prepared *marunggay* broth for her, the fever worsened. Dayaw made an offering to Apo Daga; apprehensive and frightened, he placed the bowl of glutinous rice with hard boiled eggs in the corner where she slept. The fever did not leave till a few days afterwards and she was still weak when she got up to do her work.

She was friendly; she smiled at all whom she met and to Dayaw's people and friends, she showed obeisance and respect. He was convinced, though she never admitted it, that her bearing was noble, but why, why did she go to the river? She told him afterwards that she was curious, that she would have crossed the river, too, if only she was made to run swiftly like a deer, that she had gone up the mountain often and looked at creation spread before her, the forest and the plain and beyond, the river emptying into the sea.

He finally took her there on a night when the surf was rough, a night without stars. At first, she was scared but he held her hand. Together they breasted the surf as it collapsed on them until they got to where it was calm and the water was up to their shoulders when it heaved.

He thought he could soften her loneliness if he explained, although he did not have to. "It is what you remind my people of, not what you are..." he told her.

In the soft dark, her eyes shone, the grateful smile. She chose to be elusive. "Don't worry," she said. "I can belong anywhere, I can even be across the sea although I don't know what is there..."

"But the greatest unknown, one that we can never get into, is the mind of other people," Dayaw said.

She was not meant to do all that work, to bear all those insults. She had become very thin and one afternoon, in the month when the rains were to come again, Dayaw came upon her at weaving, the shuttle unmoving in her hands. Tears were rolling down her cheeks. Dayaw was engulfed by the pity and compassion he had felt for her from the very start.

In the morning, he prepared provisions for the long walk—dried meat, rice cooked in coconut milk, salt and sugar, and the tubes of water. He told her to gather her things, nothing really but her old dress, the buffalo skin sandals that were almost frayed and the length of fabric that she had woven. They left Daya before light broke upon the land and late the following day, they finally reached the river.

All through the night, he had been quiet and now, looking at her moving quietly, a great sadness filled him. He was taking her back and he wanted to go as far as it was possible, to cross the river with her, so he waited for darkness, until the stars swarmed out of the sky. Once, she slipped over a mossy boulder and he reached out to steady her and her grasp was firm and warm.

They reached the curve at the other side, and as he had planned, headed for the cove where he had found her. After they had eaten the cold rice and the dried meat and drank from the pool, she laid on the sand the piece of cloth she had woven and they lay down. He slept easily, and at the first sliver of light, he woke up to find that she was still beside him. He watched her, the slow rise of her breast, her parted lips, her closed eyes. Then she stirred.

"I had expected you to leave in the night," he said. "Well, you know why we are here. I have caused you harm and sorrow. Also, I did not do right—from the very beginning, I know that now."

He rose, unsheathed the knife at his side and handed it to her without ceremony. "You can have your revenge now," he said simply.

Her eyes widened in amazement, in wonder. She fell on her knees, hugged his legs then kissed his feet. "Dayaw, I belong to you," she murmured.

That was how it really began. Back in Daya, in the mornings when dew was still glistening on the grass and cooking fires still sent gray smoke trailing above the houses, he would rise to find that she already had food for him. She would hover silently around, waiting for his every whim to express itself.

The first time was a revelation; she had gone with him to gather firewood in the communal forest beyond the fields; it was to be their fuel for the rainy season and she had balanced a heavy load on her head and his own load was on a pole slung over his shoulder. The day was warm and beads of sweat were on her nape like pearls.

They were about to break through into the clearing and he was tired so he brought his load down and helped her to bring her bundle down, too. She was close to him and he could smell her warm body, her hair. He drew her to the shadow of a great tree; she met his gaze without fear, without pretense. It was as if she had expected this moment, too, and with one deft pull at the knot on her shoulder, she let her dress drop so that she stood before him as he had seen her for the first time, only now there was no anxiety, no fear in her eyes.

She was not as experienced as Liwliwa and there was this unspoken demand that he teach her, but for the moment he knew only his need, the fire that must be quenched and when it was, he lay on his back, his breathing quiet and slow. The sun filtered through the leaves above them. She lay beside him, unmoving, while his hand stroked her smooth, flat belly.

"I hope I did not hurt you," he said afterwards.

"I will be better next time," she said. "I am sorry I don't know too well how to please you. And no one but you will teach me..."

She still slept in the kitchen except on those nights when he called her in, but after two months, when she was finally sure, Dayaw forbade her to sleep there for always.

That morning, before the men went to the fields or put out to sea, he put on the robe that she had woven and she slipped into her old Laud dress, and on her head a garland of *kalachuchi* that Parbangon had made. Then they went down the steps, bright with happiness.

Parbangon walked ahead of them, blowing on the buffalo horn, the shrill blasts echoing in the morning quiet. They walked hand in hand, first, to the farthest end of town, close to the sea, and the people peered out of their windows or paused in their yards to watch them. The young men smiled, but none of the girls greeted them. Liwliwa had done her work; more than that, she had cursed them.

Their march around the town ended in his father's house beside the community hall. They paused at the bottom of the flight while Parbangon blew the horn again and again.

The Ulo came out, his face glum and with a wave of his hand, he forbade the younger son to continue the bleating. To Dayaw, he said with a slow shake of his venerable head: "Now"—more in sadness than in anger—"Dayaw, you will never be Ulo."

"But I will be happy, Father," Dayaw said, looking straight at his father. Within the house, his mother was wailing; she shared her husband's sorrow and she must have wondered what terrible deed of hers had displeased Apo Langit. And that evening when Waywaya came with her offering of rice and coconut milk, Pintas accepted both, but in the presence of her daughter-in-law, she emptied the pots unto the pit where her pigs were.

Hate—this was the strongest and rawest of feelings that bound people together and it was hate, Dayaw knew, that made the Taga Daya regard Waywaya and now, himself, with derision. And how did this feeling start? How did it take root? It was in the fears and insecurities of his own people and it was the Ulo—his father—who knew how to use hate. It was he, his family and his family's relatives and friends who benefited from the largesse that hatred created. Indeed, without hate and fear, the Ulo would not have been able to shape Daya into the fortress that it had become. But at what cost?

Knowing this, Dayaw often wondered how it would be if he fled to the deeper forest. Such a flight was a wish that he sometimes played in his mind, imagined himself starting out, clearing the land with his bare hands, planting the crops on a patch that the wilderness would constantly encroach upon. The labor would be severe and the vigil constant. How to watch over the field, protect it from wild pigs, marauding deer and rats—and no fence would really keep away the wild buffaloes and when the grain was ripe, there would be the birds. How much simpler it would be if he just stayed and moved with the daily rhythm that his father had decreed. Here, there was a community, order, certitude—the finality that would assure him and everyone not only of their place but of their destiny.

How was it in other lands?

Hate and injustice were everywhere and he himself had contributed to the inequity of things. Look at what you have done to Waywaya; you do not love her, you merely possess her. You are as guilty as your father, as your warriors who have ambushed and maimed the Taga Laud.

And in the evenings, when he strummed his *kutibeng* and sang, the words were sad. Waywaya understood.

"Why are you so unhappy?" she asked.

"Because you are."

"With you I am always happy."

"And when I am no longer here?"

"I'll stand by myself," she said.

He shook his head. He had made up his mind; he would speak to the Ulo again, find out how they could clear the dust that had suffocated them. He formed clearly and sharply the thoughts that he would express:

Our roofs are lined with the skulls of our enemies and they do not evoke their ghosts to rampage in our midst, they don't disturb our sleep for their death is a joy to us. But their homes also bear the skulls of our loved ones and they are there without honor.

What has war brought us? Women wailing when they should be singing.

How much blood has been spilled? It was not used to water the crops, quench our thirst, or wash the dirt from our bodies. And the flesh of our enemies—we did not fill our stomachs with it, or make the fields fertile with it. Who knows what they who fell before our lances could have achieved, what offspring they would have sired, what clearings they would have made? All this is for the mind to guess, for the death that we bestowed unto them is final.

They walked slowly on the beach, the waves to their right dappled with moonsilver. It was a quiet night interrupted by the sounds of children playing in the moonlight, the howling of dogs; the planting season would soon set in, still no avenging warriors from Laud, still no tear in the fine fabric of peace.

"They are afraid," the Ulo said. "They cannot penetrate the wall of our determination. And if they come, will they be fast enough to flee to their sanctuary, to escape our hound dogs? Then you ask, why are we strong?"

Dayaw stared at the waves breaking on the surf with a murmur. "Nature has been on our side, Father," he said.

"Not just nature," the Ulo was exuberant. "We know our past, we don't repeat its mistakes. That, too, is tradition."

"The past could also be a prison, Father," Dayaw said. "You always look back, not ahead. Do you know that across the river, they are cooking not with the earthen pots but with copper? They have kilns, better than ours, not for making pots but for melting metals. And they have beeswax and mountain dyes. Hardwood. And their spears..."

"Our bamboo spears are lighter, easier to throw."

"Their spearheads are better."

"We fight in groups, we eat rice—not *camotes.*"

"They have lowland rice, too, and they use water from the spring..."

The Ulo was silent.

Dayaw continued evenly. "We have to change, Father. To be where we are, we have to change..."

"That is the law of life," the Ulo said. "You are not telling me anything."

"Change—not war."

"War—that is part of change. And however you may detest it, with war we have become prosperous. And I have worked very hard..."

"We have worked very hard."

"And now, our seed rice is the best in this land. Our water buffaloes are the strongest. We used our knowledge to breed, not just plants, but animals..."

"And people?"

"Don't speak like that to me."

"You wanted Liwliwa for my wife."

"Her father is powerful and..."

"The way Mother's father was powerful..."

"Yes—and everything we do should contribute to Daya, to our unity, our progress...Even our leisure. Our weaving, our pottery..."

"The Taga Laud have better..."

"That is not the test. A people survives not because of its pots. It survives, endures because it has a will..."

"And who provides the will, Father? The leaders?"

"Yes!"

"The people, Father. And that will comes when they have things they can be proud of. Not just their seed rice, their water buffaloes. The Taga Laud—they have iron plows. We need their metals and they need our salt, our fish, our fibers and our oil..."

"Self-reliance. Disclipline. These are all we need," the Ulo said. "Twenty years and look, I've given Daya new irrigation canals as well. And look at the community house that your mother built. How grand, how beautiful it is."

"And it is decorated with the skulls of our enemies."

The Ulo ignored the remark. "She has also helped the weavers, sold what they made, improved their designs. And the carvers. Has there been any time that our crafts have been so encouraged? We don't rely any more on the bowls and plates that the Narrow Eyes bring from across the sea. Soon we will be firing our own kilns and making plates just as beautiful..."

"We don't have that kind of clay, Father," Dayaw reminded him.

"Then we will get the clay where it exists. We will expand our commerce, our frontiers. The sea is not the limit, nor the mountains."

He had heard it all before and he would hear it again.

"...but to achieve all this, we need leaders with vision." He could have said, look at me! Look at me! The Ulo was describing himself, and now his voice pitched: "Cunning, courage—these are never enough. Wisdom—what one gathers through years of being human, by learning from the people and acting out their desires for truth."

But what is truth? Dayaw had asked himself many times but could not find the answer except that he believed what he felt and saw, the sunrise that gladdened him, the wind in the bamboo, the smell of new rice, of meat crackling in the open fire. And now, Waywaya—the scent of her hair, the warmth and softness of her being—he would not be leader now, not with her as his wife.

"Parbangon is growing like a bamboo shoot, Father," Dayaw said, divining his father's thoughts.

"And he is already taking after you."

"He must know poetry, and music, too. He will be a complete man." Then Dayaw said it: "So he will be the leader, Father. What I cannot be. But Waywaya—at least, you can be kind to her."

"She is Taga Laud," the Ulo said sadly.

"She is my wife. And her baby—" he said this slowly, "our baby—he will have your blood, Father!"

Dayaw watched her go through the phases, the first three months during which she hankered for oranges, for chicken as only the Taga Laud could cook, but when it was cooked—its blood coagulated with its flesh—she would have none of it. She became emaciated and he worried about her health; he gathered water buffalo milk, lots of fish and *marunggay* leaves for her. He marveled at the miracle of life in her belly, felt its first stirring. With eyes shining, she had told him of her deepest wish that the child become truly happy and not given to gloom because of her.

But why did she have to die? O Apo Langit, O Apo Daga—all of you who shape the course of time and the destiny of men, what wrong has she done? He had watched her bleed; he could not staunch the flow and there was no healer who would come. "Waywaya—you have a son!" he cried and she looked at him and smiled, then slowly, ever so slowly, she closed her eyes.

There was no wailing; only Parbangon knew Waywaya was no more. The house was quiet as it had always been. Dayaw washed her carefully and dressed her in the Taga Laud dress that she wore when he first saw her. He kissed her lips, then bundled the little thing that was his son and hastened to his father's house.

"You have a grandson, Mother," he told Pintas who met him at the stairs. "And the slave whom all of you loathed—don't waste your feelings on her anymore. She is no longer among us..."

The traces of beauty were still on her face. "It is not my fault, child of mine. It's fate," Pintas remonstrated.

"I am not blaming anyone," Dayaw said. "Not even fate. But promise me, Mother, raise my son to love his mother as I have always loved you..."

And why do you say this?"

"I have a duty to do, Mother. I'll not be there to watch him grow..."

It was then that the immensity of what he was saying struck her. She shrieked—an animal cry of surprise and grief that brought the Ulo to the house. To him, Pintas fled, her face contorted with fright. "Stop him, my husband. He does not have to do it. She was not one of us!"

"What foolishness is this?" his father asked. "Must you spite me? Whatever it is that I have done, I did because you are my blood and I want you honored..."

"I do not seek honor, Father."

"You have already shown that. But now, I want you alive, whatever your faults, whatever your weaknesses."

"Tradition, Father. We have to live up to it. You said that."

"Don't throw it back to me like spoiled meat..."

"But I believe in tradition, too, Father. This you never really understood. There are traditions we must uphold because they are not just for us—they are for all people..."

The Ulo was silent.

"How many seasons passed that she was without honor among my people? But I can honor her now."

"Then live with dishonor!" the Ulo screamed at him. "For me! Now!"

He went forward and embraced his father, tears scalding his eyes. "My son, my son," the Ulo whispered. Dayaw felt his father's arms tighten around him. It was the last time that they would embrace.

Parbangon had already been circumcised and had already started to build his own house. "She is light," Dayaw told him remembering how he carried Waywaya across the river. "I will carry her upright, strapped to my back."

"But that is not how it is done, Manong," Parbangon insisted. And of course, his brother was right.

"You are not that strong..."

Parbangon shook his head. "No, that is not the reason. You fear for me."

Dayaw did not speak; he was condemning his brother to a life of travail but Parbangon knew all that. "She was a sister to me. She cooked for me, wove for me. I have not done anything for her. Let me honor her, too."

Dayaw wrapped Waywaya in the blanket she had woven, the bright red with the blue of her people, the designs of moon, mountain and tree coming through the slats of bamboo. On both ends of the pole to which the bier was attached were the wreaths of *kalachuchi* that Parbangon had made.

They reached the river easily the following afternoon for they rested and ate but little and Dayaw marveled at the boy's strength. They untied the thongs of their sandals and waded across the shallows, stepping over mossy boulders, taking care that their precious burden did not tilt into the water. There was still plenty of light when they reached the other side and he followed the bend to the small cove where he first saw her. How peaceful it was and briefly, in his mind's eye, he saw her again as he saw her then, poised before the pool, serene as nightfall, and a sharp, almost physical pain coursed through him.

By dusk, they reached the town of Laud; they had been watched even before they had approached the fringes and now, the enemy appeared from everywhere—women, children and men who looked at them more with curiousity than hate.

He knew where to go; he had studied the town only too well and to his knowledge Waywaya had contributed her share. A clutch of women met them before they reached the clearing in front of their community hall and they started wailing, their voices high-pitched and nasal and listening to what they said—the sister, the friend who was no more—again tears dimmed his eyes. Through the blur, he could see the structure before him, the high posts with finely carved filigrees, the beams jutting out and around the rafters—just below the grass roof—a line of skulls of his people.

The huge door of the community hall swung open and down the massive wooden stairs he came, the leader of Laud, and as Dayaw had always suspected though Waywaya never confirmed it, this man with a peacock headdress and gold bracelets was Waywaya's father. He held Dayaw by the shoulder as Dayaw lowered Waywaya onto the wooden platform where offerings were made, and spoke in a voice that quavered: "It has been two harvest seasons. We missed her..." Then he beckoned to one of the older women who had met them, and to her he said. "Look at your jewel, woman!"

Darkness came quickly and with it, bird calls and the cool breezes of the mountain. He sat with the old chief in the place of honor, and they filed up to him—the warriors of Laud with their wooden shields and shiny battle axes, and raised their arms in salute. Then the gongs started beating, sonorous and loud—his knell.

Death would be welcome, for with Waywaya's passing no longer would the sky hold its dominion over him, nor would the earth that he had cultivated, whose fruits he would offer to her. How will it feel? There would be pain but he could bear that. He had been wounded before, had seen blood ooze from the wound, had felt his head grow light and his strength slowly ebb. It was not this pain which he feared for the warrior was prepared for it. It was this deeper anguish that no herb, no saucery could staunch.

All around them the huge pine splinter torches had been ignited and they cast a red glow over the crowd; it was time to do the final ceremony and they rose—just he and her family, and they formed a small procession to the side of the mountain where a hole had already been dug. They let him shove her coffin within, then they pushed a boulder at the entrance to the burial place and covered it with earth. Waywaya's mother planted before it a few strands of *ramos*—they would grow, tall and purple.

He was a Taga Daya, he must show them that he could dam his feelings but as tears streamed down his cheeks, he shuddered violently and cried. The chief laid an arm around Dayaw's shoulder and took him back.

The gongs were louder now and above their rhythm rose the squealing of pigs being butchered. They went up the hall, its floor of hewn wood, and from the roof dangled lamps of iron, ablaze with light.

"I have asked my father," Dayaw said, "that they do not cross the river anymore, that if they do, they bear gifts of life. I pray that you do the same. This is what Waywaya would have wanted..."

The old chief, squatting on his deerskin rug, did not reply; his gaze went beyond the bonfire outside the wide open door, leaping now, lighting the sombrous sky. In the yellow embroidery of flames, it seemed that his eyes were glazed and when he finally spoke, his words were slow and they bore great feeling.

"There is something about an old tree," he said; "it grows no more. At the same time, it is difficult to cut it down. Its roots are deep although it can draw no more sustenance from the earth. Maybe, it is right that new trees should grow..."

He ate little when the food finally came. Parbangon ate nothing for he had fallen asleep. They brought Dayaw wine—sweet and slightly bitter—and he wondered if it would be in the wine. But it was not.

It was late and he must rest so they left him while the feasting and dancing continued outside. He slept fitfully until dawn—that deep and tranquil quiet when just a tint of purple appeared in the east and stars still studded the sky like gems. Now, thoughts crowded his mind like drones and he was filled once more with regret that he had not been kinder to her. He could see her now in this time of day, her hair glossy and black, her precious face, the luminous eyes, the moist lips—the image of her alive and breathing and touching, pottering in the kitchen, preparing his meal. And the baby—yes, their son, how would it be when he finally became a man?

And Parbangon, would they enslave him or let him return as he had hoped they would, so that he could tell the Taga Daya? And how would it end for him? He had been trained not to fear death and though he had considered fighting, there was no sense to it as there was really no logic for his being here, just as the Ulo had said. No logic, but since when did love have any?

Morning and time to leave. The old chief was at the door as he approached. Dayaw glanced at Parbangon who was still asleep.

"Don't wake him up," the chief said softly. "He needs rest; we will take him back to the river..."

A wave of joy engulfed him. They went down the broad steps, into a brilliant morning where some of the warriors had already gathered. The old chief put an arm around his shoulder, murmuring, "Husband of my daughter—my son."

"Father of my wife, my father," he returned the farewell.

In the clear light, everything stood out now—the bamboo houses with their grass roofs, the corrals for the pigs, the chicken houses, the vegetable patches, the orange trees. He know almost everything around him just as Waywaya had described it; why, he was almost at home!

They walked him to the edge of the village. He must utter now the important word. "Waywaya," he said in reverential prayer, "I loved her. The fruit of our union—a boy. Your blood is in him, he is across the river. Will you let him grow in peace, ignorant of a time like this? Will you?"

The chief did not answer and if he spoke Dayaw did not hear. The gongs started again and then, from the women in the distance the sound of wailing. Was it for him? In his heart, though he was afraid, he was glad. The forest awaited him but as sure as sunset he knew that he would not reach the river.

Born in 1924 in the Philippines, F. Sionil José is grateful to two teachers: Soledad Oriel, a grade school teacher who lent books to him, and Paz Latorena, a university professor who encouraged him to write. His work has been published internationally and has been translated into several languages. In 1958 he founded the Philippine Center of International PEN. In 1980 he received the Ramon Magsaysay Award for journalism, literature and creative communication arts. "Waywaya" won first prize in the most prestigious literary competition in the Philippines, the Annual Palanca Memorial Awards.

"Folk working like mad to get the hay in in time, and here we read a book. Where's the logic of it?"

Inglés

BY MARIA NUROWSKA

IT'S there being no dos and don'ts that's the main thing. To saunter down the lane, say. The wood on your left, the Grzegota meadow on your right. A pretty meadow, too, always full of cowslips, in the ditch, especially, because it dries out last.

Now she was free to crop her hair as short as necessary. Nobody would stare. She could stand in the middle of the road and shout at the top of her voice: "Shit!" She'd always liked strong language, only it was forbidden. Not now, though. She could stand and shout at the top of her voice, even here in the middle of the road.

How would she look with her hair cut short, she wondered. It ought to be all right, but either way, it wasn't her now, was it? So it wouldn't make any particular difference.

Everything could have taken a different turn five years ago when that came to her. But she knew it was a matter of time and all she had to do was wait. And she hadn't been wrong.

Throw off her sandals and walk over the warmed sand. Feel it softly under her feet. That's when that comes to her. The smell of heather, the sun on her face, shining straight into her eyes, making her close them tight. And everything red, orange, gold-red from the sun. And the face of Inglés, the face of Inglés...

Grzegota dropped the rake and looked round the hayfield.

"It's no good," he said to his son, "we won't rake it all."

"What do you know! Wladek's become a glutton for work. Shout it from the housetops!"

"It's going to rain, they said in the village."

"Come on, come on, there's the book to be read," the father insisted. Wladek shouldered his rake and led the way. They had reached the first farmyards when he addressed his father:

"You've gone clean out of your mind, Pa, with that reading. Just like that cracked Marta."

"Now, now, don't you be so smart-alecky," his father replied. "You're to do as your Pa says, and you won't go wrong."

"I ask you! Folk working like mad to get the hay in in time, and here we read a book. Where's the logic of it?"

"Let them. If my ideas work out, the hay'll be no loss."

Wladek made no answer, but merely spat into the nettles by the ditch and turned off towards the house.

He was in the mood to go into the village, but his father at once took the book out of the trunk in which he put it away for the night and told him to carry on reading.

"Slowly, mind," he admonished his son. "Don't rush because I want to be sure of getting everything right."

"Where had we got to?" Wladek asked.

"I marked the place, didn't I?" his father said, settling himself comfortably on a chest by the stove.

She lay down on the bed fully dressed. Fat flies crawled over the ceiling, their corseted, yellowish bellies gleaming. One of them suddenly took off and, after circling the room, landed on the very middle of the flypaper.

"Serve you right," Marta crowed.

The fly buzzed intolerably. Eventually it began desperately trying to free itself from the trap. Its legs stuck in the glue as it struggled back and forth, from one end of the flypaper to the other.

"You're a game thing," Marta shook her head. She got up off the bed and taking the fly gently behind the wings helped it get free.

"Fly away! I'm sparing your life."

She went over to the window. The haymakers were coming home. The women were chattering away, but when they saw Marta in the window, conversation died at once.

Presently one of them said:

"What do you suppose the chit's going to do with that money!"

She took her coat off the hanger and went outside.

It had turned dark. From the fields came an evening chill mixed with the smell of cut grass.

After an hour the father closed his eyes and his head began to nod, but when Wladek broke off, he at once said:

"What have you stopped for? I'm listening!"

Wladek sighed and began to read on.

Marta reached the bridge beyond which stretched the Grzegota meadow. It was the only one which hadn't been all mown. In some places the grass grew waist-high. The thick blades caught on her coat and curled round her legs. She lay down on the ground, her head tilted. She breathed the smell of heather crushed. The sun began to shine straight into her eyes and made her close them tight. And everything was red, orange, gold-red from the sun. And above her the face of Inglés and the weight of his body, his hands.

She got to her feet, her teeth chattering, her coat crumpled and bedewed. Why? Why was she forever alone?

The next day it began to rain.

"The hay will be spoiled, that's for sure," Wladek moaned. "Hadn't we better get it into the barn, even though it's wet?"

"That's no good," the father shook his head. "It might catch fire. Leave it lying where it is. The rain may not last, and we can spread it then. There's no point going out of doors. Better get on with the reading."

They read until noon when Wladek stretched and said:

"Knocking-off time!"

"Don't give me that," the father snorted. "We've got to finish today."

"We just have."

"What do you mean?" he snapped. "Read me that last sentence again."

He could feel his heart beating against the pine needle floor of the forest.

"Does it then say 'The End'?"

"No, but there's a dash. In any case, it's obviously the end."

"How so?"

"The officer will ride up, he'll open fire and the troopers will do him in."

"It doesn't say that there, does it?"

"But, Pa, you don't write everything in books...you leave a bit to be guessed."

"But it doesn't say that there, does it? So how do you know for sure they'll do him in? Suppose it's the other way round and it's him that does them in."

"It couldn't be, because he hasn't enough ammunition."

Grzegota shook his head.

"In other words he does get done in!"

"That's it."

"But I don't suppose it's for getting him done in she wants that Inglés."

"What are you jabbering about?"

"Jabbering. As if you didn't know. Marta's waiting for her Inglés and it looks to me you could fit the part easy."

Wladek was lost for words.

"Why should I want to?" he stammered at last.

"Because she's now the prize catch in the village, that's why."

"But everyone knows she's soft in the head."

"Maybe, but look how many of them have tried to play the Inglés? None of them took her fancy. But we've read the book and we know how to go about it."

Wladek turned away from his father.

"Well, son, cat got your tongue?"

"What's there to say? You know I'm going steady already..."

"But, son, that girl you're after hasn't a bean. How many of them are there on those few acres?"

"Getting rich isn't what I'm interested in," Wladek growled.

The father tried to talk him round, but he wouldn't hear of calling on Marta.

"If you're so keen on that money of hers, why don't you go round yourself? You're a bachelor, too, aren't you!"

"Not a bachelor, chump, only a widower."

"What does that matter? Didn't Antczak marry last year? He was a widower, too, and two years older than you."

The old man paced the room, turning something over in his mind.

"There's none so deaf..." he muttered.

Wladek surreptitiously took his cap off the peg and hurried out.

The father didn't stop him. He took a mirror out of a drawer and inspected his features.

"It wouldn't be a bad idea to blacken up the whiskers a bit," he said out loud.

He found some blacking. At once he looked younger. Then he stripped off his shirt and threw out his chest.

"You're turning gray," he shook his head. He thought of blackening the hair on his chest as well, but dropped the idea. He tried on his jacket. It looked sort of tight. No good at all. In any case it stood to reason Ingléses didn't go around in jackets. In the end he put on Wladek's black polo-neck, which was also a little tight because he was broader in the shoulders than his son, but at least made him look slimmer than he was.

He inspected himself in the mirror once more and went out, leaving the key behind the door-frame in case Wladek came home early.

It was still raining.

"The hay's sure to be spoiled, which will be money down the drain, but if things go well with Marta, there'll be bigger pickings. I'd build me a brick pig-sty and we could increase the stock by half, which would be sheer profit. And the barn's old, the roof likely to cave in any minute."

So musing, he reached the parish hall where Marta was still living though the materials for building a house had already been collected.

In front of the door he got cold feet and couldn't make himself go in. But when he thought of all that hay going to waste his blood stirred and he knocked.

In due course he heard steps on the stairs and then Marta asked: "Who's there?"

"Inglés," the old man answered.

There was a moment of complete silence on the other side and then the bolt creaked back.

Grzegota stepped inside.

They eyed each other. Marta was standing in a ray of light coming from a half-opened door upstairs. Her hair was cropped short. She was surprised it was Grzegota of all people. But when she took a closer look at his figure, she saw that he had strong, broad shoulders and was slim and lithe for a man his age. He attracted her with that black moustache and thick hair combed to one side. Yes, he could be Inglés.

"Let's go upstairs," she whispered.

They climbed the stairs and the girl opened the door wide. The flood of light was so bright it made them blink.

For a moment he wondered if he could cope with that Inglés, but she had already entered and stood by the window.

The first thing he did was to press the switch. Then in one motion he pulled off his sweater and stepped over to the girl.

He touched her back. It felt thin. He ran his fingers over the protruding shoulder-blade and a lump came into his throat.

She turned round. The whole of her face was in shadow; only her hair glistened. He stretched out his hand and touched her face. Before he knew it he had whispered:

"Little squirrel."

"Rabbit," she corrected him, but it's doubtful whether he heard at all.

For both of them had definitely ceased to be themselves, only Marta had known that earlier and he had found out only now as she stood there in the dark, her hair glistening.

She closed her eyes and bent forward, then knelt down in front of Grzegota and pressed her face against his knees. He could feel her warm breath through his trousers. He knew what he should do now, only he was limp. His arms dangled helplessly, his knees started to tremble.

"If I don't get a hold of myself, she'll throw me out double quick. Yet by the looks of it I seem to have worked as Inglés. All because of that fasting...I'd forgotten how it is with women and I may not cope." A feeling of pity swept over him at failing to cope now when everything was shaping up so promisingly. He'd help Wladek set up on his own...Fancy wanting to marry that girl who was poor as a church mouse. It was six years since he'd been with a woman and now he'd never cope. He wanted to get dressed and rush out, but Marta pulled him down on the floor and began unfastening his belt.

"There's a hook and eye down there," he said hoarsely.

He had trouble finding it himself even though he knew where it was sewn. Marta, however, found it sooner.

Her fingers roamed impatiently over him. She was in a hurry. In her nostrils was the smell of heather crushed and the sun began to shine straight into her eyes so that she had to close them ever tighter.

"Come, Inglés, come, come," she whispered frantically.

And the old man now felt that from her pleading and her roaming fingers his limpness was going. Everything in him began to stiffen, grow, swell. He felt strong and raising himself on the elbows grasped Marta around the waist. He clutched her tighter while she trembled, whispering over and over: "Come, Inglés, come..."

"Wait...Let me look at you...You're so lovely." He had never spoken like that to anyone ever before, but then he had never been Inglés, never been so sure of his strength. There had been times with his woman when he couldn't. He'd get worked up, but at the last movement go limp. But today he knew he'd cope with that Inglés; his legs had stopped trembling.

He would have gone on looking, but Marta lifted her arms and pulled him down on top of her.

And he could feel the bursting stalks of heather scratching his flesh, digging into his skin, causing pain. Nothingness opened before him and he rushed in headlong.

Out of the corner of his eye he saw it was happening to Marta too. Her head was thrown back and she was beating it against the bent stalks of heather. He noticed a vein throbbing on her throat and he wanted to touch the spot with his lips, but it was too late. Like Marta he, too, was blinded by the sun and he began to writhe and tremble convulsively while she clasped his neck in a tight embrace.

Later he was afraid of opening his eyes. He was sure now it was not the heather of a mountain meadow in Spain, but the floor of the parish hall on the hill. He had no idea what Marta would say. He was ashamed of her and his nakedness. He was not used to it. His old woman had thought it the end of the world if he sometimes tried to pull her nightshirt up a little higher.

Cover himself in front of Marta, get dressed and clear out. But he was scared to move. He could feel the girl's shoulder under his neck. It was motionless, frightening.

When she stirred, he tucked his head into his shoulder as though shrinking from a blow.

But she was saying something softly. Then he realized she was asking him to stroke her head.

At first he was astonished that it was still going on and then something began bursting him open from the inside and but for shame before Marta he might perhaps have wept.

He stretched out his hand and began stroking her head. The close-cropped hair yielded gently to his touch and he knew she had only to ask and he would do anything for her, die, sell his land, become a hired laborer.

But she didn't want anything like that. All she said was that it was cold and they'd best climb under the blanket.

They lay there in the dark, Marta's head on his chest.

He ought to have questioned her thoroughly about that legacy, but it seemed to matter so little. She could be as penniless as before, when she'd been the village librarian.

But since he wanted to do right by Wladek, he said:

"There's a new sty needs building."

"We'll build one," she whispered.

Maria Nurowska, born in 1944, is a graduate of the University of Warsaw. Her first collection of short stories, Nie strzelaj do organisty, *was published in 1975. She has also published novels and has written for television and radio. Her story "The Codger" was in SSI No. 25.*

“I couldn’t believe the nun didn’t realize we were faking.”

Give and Take

BY PAUL DOBSON

I hesitated as I held out the white sticker with the red printing that said: Sisters of Charity Collection for Orphans.

“Perhaps you’d better stick it on yourself,” I said, feeling spare. I mean, all she had on top was a thin bit of material that made things obvious. But I suppose it was a hot day and everybody was gay and cheerful, doing their last-minute shopping for Christmas.

She smiled back at me, in a cheeky way, as if she was daring me. She probably didn’t need the excuse of the heat to dress in a way that turns young guys like me on. Normally, I’d have a go, but I couldn’t help remembering the old nun with the shining face saying: “Ah, thank you, Mr. Brogan. You are very kind. I am sure you will be blessed.” Also I didn’t want to mess up the whole plan just because I couldn’t control my urges. I mean, the guys would never forgive me. So I just held out the sticker.

She put her head to one side and smiled at me as if she’d won. She pressed the sticker neatly on to her top and went off with a waggle, all high heels and shorts and long tanned legs. Well, I mean, they were hardly even shorts. Some people ask for trouble.

Three little kids put in a cent each and took my mind off her. I stuck stickers on them while they giggled a bit.

I suppose the old nun thought the four of us really were good Catholic boys, with names like O'Reilly, O'Conner, Quinlan, and Brogan. Actually, it was Gavin's idea. He had been to CBC for a while till he got expelled, and the names really belonged to four of the Brothers who had been at the school then.

A thin dark bloke came up. He really looked tough, with tattoos on his arms, a knitted jelly-bag on his head, and a dirty chain round his neck. He was scruffy, but you could have knocked me over with a feather when he put two 20-cent pieces into the box. You can always see what they put in, you know. I stuck a sticker on him and said "Thank you." He probably thought I sounded pious, but actually I was amazed. I mean, I had never put a cent into a collection box in my life.

All the larks were always Gavin's idea. He'd overheard two blokes talking on the train on the way home from town and told us about it.

"John, I've been wanting to get round to asking you something," the one man had said, all posh. They were both wearing suits and the one had a briefcase. "I wondered if you would help with a street collection on Saturday morning. Sister Dominic phoned me today at the office. Apparently Christmas Eve is a great time to be allowed a collection, but they are short of volunteers."

"Heavens, Peter," said the man with the briefcase. "I'd rather run the Two Oceans Marathon. But I suppose you can't say no to the sisters. What do I have to do?"

"Pick up a box from one of them—they'll be in the car park behind Woolworths. They'll tell you where to stand. If you can get someone else to come along too, it'll be a big help."

A huge woman with loads of parcels stopped in front of me. Slowly, she took out her purse and produced ten cents as though she was thinking about it a lot. She seemed a bit shy when she put it in the box. I gave her a sticker and she said, "Thank you, master."

Gavin had done all the talking in the car park. He really can put it on when he wants to. "Thank you, sister. No, it's a pleasure, sister. Don't worry, sister—we're quite happy to do more than an hour, sister." We had to tell her our names and she wrote them down with a fountain pen on a list of the box numbers. She took ages to find the boxes and check them.

A tall, thin man with a hat and walking-stick came up to me. He didn't hold out money, just said: "Young man, I should like you to know that I find it totally abhorent that a collection for the Church of Rome should be allowed in this city, specially at Christmas time."

And off he went, all stiff and uptight. I'm no Catholic but I could have clocked him one. Who the hell did the old pansy think he was, anyway? At least the old nun had been polite.

We'd had to sign our names next to where she'd written them down. Poor old Bill had to sign Quinlan, but he was sharp enough to put down such a scrawl that it could just as well have been Van der Merwe. At least Brogan was easier, but I felt a fool writing it down. I couldn't believe the nun didn't realize we were faking.

I was starting to feel fed up standing there. It was getting hotter and there were more people. They all jumbled along at different speeds and different angles, all looking straight ahead. Some even walked into me. People are crazy. I mean, some of them stared at me but most definitely didn't look at me. Some kind of flaunted the fact that they were already wearing stickers. I disliked them less than the ones who didn't look at me, I suppose.

I wasn't enjoying myself. I mean, a guy feels spare. I know I don't look like a goody goody, even when I try. What would have happened if someone who really knew me came along? Gavin said that was a risk we'd have to take, and who was to say we hadn't been converted, anyway? Also, it was a long way from Bellville and people in Bellville had their own shops and didn't go to Claremont on Christmas Eve.

A small woman came straight up to me. Well, she came as straight as she could, as she brought her thin body along on two crutches. She moved in sections, like somebody swimming very badly.

She stopped and took a rand coin from her purse and put it into the tin.

"Happy Christmas," she said, smiling as if she had just got a present. "And God bless you for doing this for the poor children."

I said: "Same to you." What else could a bloke say? I didn't even say that easily. And I held out a sticker.

She said: "No, thank you. It's all right." And she smiled and went away.

It was as if somebody had punched me in the stomach when I wasn't expecting it. That old doll with the thin body on the crutches was even worse than the old nun with the shiny face. I mean, it wouldn't be so easy to slide away with the collection box and break it open with her rand in it. I'm no holy joe, but I've got some feelings.

Feeling really lousy, I tried to push the rand into the box. I suppose they were old boxes and they weren't made for rand coins. I couldn't fish it out, either: it was too far down. I tried banging the box but that didn't help. I got a 50-cent piece out of my pocket and used it to push the bigger coin in. Suddenly the rand moved and my coin followed it into the box.

Funny, I've thought about it since. I wonder if it did really slip out of my fingers. I suppose it did, because like I said, I'm no holy joe; I've never put money in a collection box, and why would I start now?

All sorts of other people came and put money in willingly. They didn't have to. Nobody made them. My little stickers were maybe worth something in pride, but there are lots of other ways you can be proud. Maybe some of them thought they were buying salvation, but none of them looked holy or anything.

Gavin said we should go down to the station, slide through the subway and meet at the car park on the other side. We could make a quick getaway to his place where he had a hammer and chisel waiting to open the tins. It would be a piece of cake, he said.

An old bloke and his wife, both short and fat and sweating, came and put a couple of coins in the box and I gave them both stickers. They were very serious about it.

Gavin said it would buy us a few beers and a lot of laughs. Who knows, there may even have been quite a bit of dough in the boxes. People get carried away at Christmas, he said.

I must say I wasn't finding it all that funny now. Nor were people getting carried away. It surprised me how stingy there were. I mean Christmas is supposed to be about giving, isn't it?

The fat bloke and his wife came past me again. As they approached, she felt for her sticker. It wasn't there and she looked all embarrassed as she went past without putting anything in.

Then this other nun came up to me. She was different—short and young, with big eyes. Her face was beautiful—not beautiful because she had tried to make it beautiful, but just open and bright and confident. I had never seen a young nun before.

She came bouncing up to me in her white gear, all cool, and said: "Your hour is up now. You must be very tired, standing here in the heat of the sun. I'll take over from you."

She had a box in her hand with a card sticking up behind it. So I said: "What do I do with this one, sister?"

"Just take it back to Sister Dominic behind Woolworths. And bless you for helping us. Happy Christmas."

I took it back to Sister Dominic behind Woolworths. She took it from me in her crooked old hands, as if I had brought her some wonderful gift. She ticked my name off. "There you are, Mr. Brogan," she said. "Bless you a thousand times. I hope you have a very happy Christmas now, you and all your family. I can tell you that all the sisters and all the children will be praying for you at Christmas Mass."

I went down to the station and caught a train to Salt River and then another out to Bellville. I spent the afternoon fixing the wheel on my mom's wheelchair—something she'd been nagging me to do for a long time.

I sort of kept to myself for a while but when I did see the others again, nobody mentioned collection boxes. I was glad of that 50 cent piece of mine.

Paul Dobson was born in 1935 in Cape Town and educated there by the Marist Brothers. He is a schoolmaster and writer, with an abiding passion for rugby football, who enjoys amateur dramatics "if farces fall into that category." Mr. Dobson has played an active role in opposition politics in South Africa "with increasing disillusionment." He was first introduced in SSI No. 14 with "The Old Boy."

"But when she opened her eyes
and could see that it was not a joke . . ."

The Arrival of Autumn in Constantinople

BY NORBERTO LUIS ROMERO

HE got out of bed and, as everyday, took a hot shower. Water, as always, filled his ears. It was when he tried to clear them that he noted it. First he thought that he was still asleep and dreaming, then that it was a mistake, false information transmitted to a brain still sluggish from rising too early. He tested it again and a cold sweat mixed with the hot water.

Slowly, with fear, he peered into the blurred mirror, where his confused silhouette materialized. He cleared the crystal surface with the palm of his hand, and that other hand met his. There he could see himself clearly, and he shuddered, raising both hands to his head and pressing at his ears.

He went to his bedroom. His wife was sleeping. He would have liked to wake her; cry out to her that he no longer had them, that he had lost them; ask her to help him prove that he was not dreaming. But he felt ashamed and kept silent, seated beside her. Tears fell from him. He wiped his eyes with an edge of the sheet and then he saw it, half-hidden under the pillow, rather transparent; without bitterness he picked it up—it was one of his ears. He looked for the other and found it on the floor.

When he had them both, in an instinctive if futile action, he tried to put them back on. He shut himself in the bathroom and there he observed them with care: they were not bleeding, they were as if withered and fragile. Again he looked at himself in the mirror and felt ridiculous. Several times he modeled his previous image, when he was whole, sustaining his ears with his fingertips. Also, in a fit of unconsciousness, he tried them on backwards and on various parts of his face. Then he grew serious.

Again he found himself sitting beside his wife, his head wrapped in a towel.

"Susanna," he called softly, "Susanna, are you awake?"

She responded with a murmur.

"My ears fell off," he said, very sadly, removing the towel.

"I'm not surprised. Autumn began three days ago."

But when she opened her eyes and could see that it was not a joke, when she saw her husband's head, oval and without those protuberances, with those two small holes, very round and almost obscene, one on either side of his head, she grew somewhat faint.

They concealed the matter from the children and told them he had struck his head in the shower, slid and fallen. But the children looked at the bandage with mistrust, as if suspecting they were lying. Marcelita began to cry.

They kept the ears in a little box which they hid in a larger box in the bureau. At night they mutually startled each other, out of bed and spying on the ears in silence, observing them without bitterness, rather with curiosity and surprise. The ears kept shrinking and wrinkling more each day. One night they discovered that moths were consuming them. Susanna washed them and put moth crystals in the box.

For three days—since Manuel's ears had fallen off—they had been phoning excuses to his office.

"Sooner or later you'll have to go to the office or call a doctor and get over your shame."

He refused. Finally she convinced him to telephone a doctor friend of his. The secretary said the doctor had been out of his office for two days. There was no other alternative than to call the social welfare doctor to give him an excuse to present at work.

"They'll laugh at me. 'I certify that Mr. So-and-so cannot go to work because he has lost his ears . . .' No, we won't call him. Besides, my ears don't hurt, they don't even bother me, and I don't miss them."

"Well, I can't call and say, 'Doctor, I'm calling you to come take a look at my husband, whose ears have fallen off . . .' "

So they decided to lie and call him concerning a bad ache in his ears. The secretary advised Susanna to wait a few days or consult another doctor because the doctor had appointments for days in advance and could not see him. Manuel was glad, but his wife insisted:

"One of these days you'll have to take off that ridiculous bandage and go outside, we'll tell the children the truth, and you'll go back to the office before they fire you."

One morning Martha called to ask how they all were. Susanna noticed she sounded somewhat nervous; it was evident Martha wanted to tell her something. Susanna did not quite understand. She herself was about to tell Martha about Manuel and ask her advice, but she did not because he was listening and at that moment Marcelita came in crying and asking her father to put her ears back on her head. She was carrying the ears in one hand like a tremulous, recently caught butterfly.

Shame and fear overcome, they called a doctor and hid nothing from him. Through him they found out that everyone in the city had lost his ears with the arrival of autumn. The next day Susanna's and Gustavito's fell off at the very same moment. They were no longer frightened. They put all the family ears together in the little box with Manuel's; Susanna arranged them in cotton and added fresh moth crystals.

At first, like Susanna and Manuel, the citizens of Constantinople shut themselves in, ashamed of their round, smooth heads, but with time, when everyone learned that being earless was universal, they began to go out, return to their jobs and to daily life. They wore hats or caps or berets fitted close to where the ears had been, but then they abandoned hats and bandannas and went out with their heads uncovered. As natural, for a while there were indiscreet glances and sly giggles, but people gradually adjusted and lack of ears even came to be aesthetic. Only children, with their natural malice, went on making fun.

The shopkeepers, who had no need of tact in Constantinople, sawed off the manequin's ears and withdrew from their show windows all modes of dress once worn by women with ears. Hair styles became short again, combed naturally. They had learned that ears are no more than capricious organs with no utility, but, curiously, a new science dedicated to the study of ears arose.

And this event, inoffensive and unimportant in appearance as the loss of ears in Constantinople may be, had its reverberations in certain aspects of the citizens' thought: dried fruit, particularly peach slices, they stopped eating because it struck them as not very ethical, almost immoral. There were also changes in the economic aspect: two ear muff factories went bankrupt. The industrial design of eyeglasses was forced to revert to old models of pincenez and monocles. National Hat Factory stock went up five and a half points during the first days of autumn. All editions of the life of Van Gogh were sold out. And fashion design did the impossible to impose the use of earrings in noses and on other parts of the face.

In parks and streets, mounds of fallen leaves which were piled up daily to be burned varied slightly in size.

Autumn was nearly over and part of winter in a tranquil and routine city like Constantinople. The residents recovered their rhythm and habits. Despite the citizens' habitual joy, numerous almanacs could be found in their houses, where people were secretly marking off the passing days. They were awaiting the arrival of spring, the singing birds, flowers, and the leaves which would once more cover the bare trees.

Norberto Luis Romero writes short stories and novels. He is a specialist in cinema, especially in animated cartoons. Mr. Romero holds dual citizenship in Spain and Argentina. His skilled translator is H.E. Francis who is also a published short story writer.

"I want to go! Please, Kamjorn, let me go!"

The Operation

BY PENSRI KIENGSIRI

ONE morning, in the Bangkok Rehabilitation Center for Crippled Children, Danu Thamrongsakdi, an eight-year-old polio victim, pushed himself over the floor towards a ten-year-old friend. Using one wasted hand to arrange his limp legs and deformed feet more comfortably he said:

"You know, I am going in for my operation on Monday!"

"Are you really?"

"Yes, Miss Ubol told me." He meant the superintendent of the Center.

"I have been waiting so long. But suddenly now it is my turn; I'm not a bit happy."

"Why? asked Pitak. His deformities were less severe. He had already learnt to walk on crutches.

"I'm scared."

"So are we all. But if you get your legs straightened, maybe you will able to walk with crutches like me; much better than having to push yourself along the floor on your arms."

"But I'm still afraid, because it will hurt."

"You said your mother would come down from the North to be near you for your operation. Is she coming?"

"I hope so! I do hope so! When my sister Darunee comes to see me today I'll ask her to write to Mother at once to make sure that she comes."

Early that afternoon, Darunee, a young girl in her teens who attended a Bangkok boarding school, stood by her brother's bed and promised, her face solemn:

"Yes, Danu. Of course I will write to Mother. But she promised she would come to Bangkok for your operation. I'll send her a telegram as soon as I leave you, because today is already Wednesday!"

Next day, in Lampang, in the far North, Danu's mother wept over Darunee's telegram.

"I am so happy for poor Danu. You will let me go to him, won't you?"

Her husband glanced up from his dinner. "How about the baby, Sriprai?"

"But you are here."

"I have the shop to look after."

"It's not every day that someone comes in to buy a radio! And there's the baby amah. I have not seen Danu once since we put him in that rehabilitation center!" She was ready to cry. Her eyes were moist.

"How about you staying with the baby, and minding the shop? I will go to Bangkok instead." His mind strayed to other days in Bangkok, student days, and to the old schoolmates he would have a chance to look up.

She hesitated, murmuring doubtfully, "It might be better if I went."

"It will certainly be better for the baby if you stay. After all, Danu is eight years old, not eight months, like the baby!"

"I know why you want to go," she thought bitterly, her heart aching for her crippled son. "You long for the bright lights. You always will, as long as you live! You are not thinking of your poor little boy. You are thinking of the fun you can have in the city. You never did care much for Danu. Where he is concerned, it is a matter of 'out of sight, out of mind!' You act as if you had only two children, Darunee and the baby. Never mind the crippled one. What's a cripple, after all? Let him live and die in the rehabilitation center where he belongs!"

"Why are you crying?"

"I want to go! Please, Kamjorn, let me go!"

"What help would you be? You're not a doctor!"

"But at least I can try to cheer Danu up before he goes in for his operation. I can give him all my love and tenderness. I can comfort him, and tell him it will be worth the pain in the end. 'Your mother is here with you. Don't be afraid.' "

"Do you think I cannot do this just as well?"

"You are a man, Kamjorn. There are things a woman can do better than a man, just as there are things a man can do better than a woman."

"Look, my dear, I give you my word. I will be at the hospital before Danu goes into the operating theater. I will do my best to comfort him. After all, he is my son too, you know. Do you think I don't love him?"

She looked at him doubtfully and pleaded one last time. "It was I who promised to be with him for his operation."

"What difference does it make? He will be delighted to see either one of us."

Friday morning, Kamjorn dressed with care and boarded the Bangkok Express. He reached the city the next day at noon. Instead of going directly to his daughter or to the rehabilitation center, he called on Aneg, his best friend.

By Sunday morning, when Darunee had seen no sign of her mother, nor received any message from home, she rang up the center to find out if her mother had been there. When the answer was negative, Darunee, upset, asked to talk to her brother Danu.

Danu burst into tears over the telephone and insisted that he would not have the operation unless he saw his mother before he went into the operating theater. The poor boy fell into a fit of hysterical weeping. It was all Miss Ubol could do to calm him.

Darunee, knowing that there was no train from Lampang due to arrive in Bangkok that day, sat in stunned silence for a few minutes. The next express train from Lampang would not arrive until noon on Monday, and the operation was scheduled for 9:00 a.m. the same day. Her mother could not possibly be in time now.

Darunee sat back, thinking hard. Danu was to have a series of operations before he gained the use of both legs. If he missed his chance of an operation this time, he would have to wait months before his turn came round again. But perhaps she could persuade Danu to have his operation, if she promised him that his mother would be with him when he woke up? She had to do something right away! It was worth trying.

Before long she was speaking to her mother on a long distance line. She left Sriprai cold with fear, anxiety and foreboding!

"Maybe Kamjorn did not get off the train at Bangkok? Did he not realize how Danu needs us? Maybe he was robbed or murdered? Or run over on the street?" There was no time to think out these terrifying thoughts. She had to pack and get going right away!

With trembling hands brushing back the tears, she threw a few pieces of clothing into a suitcase. Kissing the baby, she promised him, in her heart, to return soon. She exhorted the nursemaid to take good care of him. Then she rushed to the railway station, and boarded the Express exactly three minutes before the whistle blew.

In the train, torn between anguish over Danu, and anxiety over the baby, she shed many silent tears. In between she prayed that Danu would undergo the operation. She prayed fervently, madly.

That evening, Darunee was startled when her father visited her at her boarding school. She *wai-ed* him, putting the palms of her hands up high and together and asked:

"Father, when did you arrive?"

"Yesterday, about midday. Why?"

"I thought you had not got here! Why didn't you call me straight away, Father?"

"I met an old friend, and he took me off to the beach to relax a while. There is plenty of time, isn't there?"

"I...I think so. But Father, this morning Danu cried so much because he thought neither you nor mother would come to see him. We know there is no train or plane coming in today, but there is one leaving Lampang today. Danu said he would not let the surgeon touch him, and I was so worried that I called Mother long distance."

Kamjorn gave a light-hearted laugh. "Never mind, my dear. Your mother knows I am here. Let's go and see Danu."

That night, Kamjorn slept comfortably in his hotel, feeling well-pleased with himself. He had seen Danu's face light up when the boy saw him; in spite of the fact that he had snatched a pleasant evening at Pattaya Beach, he was still in time for the operation.

"A lot of fuss about nothing," though Kamjorn. "Women!"

Next morning, outside an operating theater in one of the best hospitals in Bangkok, Kamjorn held his little son in his arms. He was telling him how wonderful it would be for all of them when the leg deformities were corrected, and Danu could walk, even on crutches. He told the boy that it would undoubtedly be painful after the anaesthetic had worn off, but that it would be worth it all in the end.

"Just think how happy Mother will be to be able to take you places! You know that she wanted to come here to you? But I wished to come and see you too, and one of us had to be with your baby brother."

"Father, can I go home after this operation? It is a year now since you brought me here. I miss Mother very much. And I have not even seen the baby."

"If it won't hurt you, and the surgeon allows it, surely, my son."

"Mother might be here today," Danu murmured hopefully. "Do you know that Darunee telephoned home yesterday? Darunee told me that Mother said she might come."

Kamjorn stroked the small arm that hung limply on his lap. "Well, she might, although I doubt it, because of the baby. However, if she does come, the four of us will go to a cowboy movie, eh? What do you say to that, little fellow, eh?"

"O, Father, you are so kind! It will be so wonderful! I have a feeling that Mother will be here, you know. I will be so happy if after the operation, I find her out here with you."

Miss Ubol, the superintendent, and a hospital orderly approached them, the orderly pushing a wheeled stretcher in front of him. Danu held his father's hand a long while before he allowed them to wheel him away on the stretcher. Kamjorn followed the boy as far as he could, turning back only after Danu had disappeared around a private-looking corner.

Suddenly, his attention was caught by two young nurses, walking towards him. They were talking about a train accident. The Northern Express, due to arrive in Bangkok at noon that day! It seemed that the accident had happened the previous evening.

For some unknown reason, Kamjorn felt a sudden quickening of his heart. Swift as lightning, his thoughts flew to his wife. He stepped up to the nurses and asked if there were fatalities.

"Fatalities?" one of them asked politely. "Oh, Yes! They said on the radio that fifty people were killed. Twenty-three have already been identified. Get today's newspaper and you will see the names."

"Names? My wife—what if she was on that Express! What will I do if her name is one of the twenty-three?" He was terrified. When the nurses told him that the newspaper they had read was in a room nearby he dashed, full of fear, to read it.

A woman doctor spotted Kamjorn's unconscious body. She had him taken to the Emergency Room and treated for shock. When he came to, he wept shamelessly, and tried to take his own life.

He was placed under the constant surveillance of a firm-lipped nurse and a stout orderly.

Word spread throughout the hospital of the deranged man whose wife had died in the train crash. Miss Ubol took one look at the man. She was horrified at Kamjorn's disheveled appearance. Suddenly her heart contracted with pity for her little crippled boy. It was not enough to be badly crippled; now Danu had lost his mother as well, just when he needed her most!

Miss Ubol urged the raving Kamjorn to get a grip on himself and think of his son, who would be coming out of the operating theater any moment. Finally, she succeeded in pacifying him, and at last the news came that the boy's operation had been successful.

Kamjorn endured agony, waiting for his son to regain consciousness. As soon as Danu was wheeled out, pale and pathetically tiny on the trolley, one of his legs encased in a plaster cast, Kamjorn ran over, and hugged him fiercely, crying:

"My baby! Oh, my baby!"

Tears were streaming down his face. Danu looked up, shocked and puzzled.

"Whatever's the matter, Father?"

"Nothing, son, nothing!"

"Are you quite sure, Father?"

"Sure, sure! How are you feeling, little fellow?"

Danu tried manfully to brave the raw nagging pain.

"It...it isn't so bad, Father. Really."

Then he looked around, "Where's Mother?" Didn't she come?"

"No!"

"Are you sure, Father?"

"Yes, dear. Why do you ask?"

"On my way out, I heard people talking about a train crash. They said this train was coming from the North, and that lots of people died in the crash. I was worried because Darunee said that Mother might be coming on that express train."

"But she did not! She did not!"

"Are you quite sure, Father?"

"I checked, darling! I've just checked!"

"Then Mother was not on that train?"

"No, she was not."

"Then Mother's not dead?"

"No, my darling! No!"

Kamjorn broke down and buried his face in the boy's hair. Danu was crying too. He hugged his father and cried for joy. With the tears running down his cheeks, he sobbed joyfully:

"Thank God! Thank God, my mother is not dead!"

Pensri Kiengsiri, from Southern Thailand, writes short stories, film epics, television serials, magazine serials and novels. Many of her stories show her attention to detail and matter-of-fact humor which distinguish her among Thai writers today. She first appeared in SSI No. 8 with "One Good Turn."

"Ethan began to experience the unsettling sensation of seeing things as he had never before seen them."

The Grand Illumination

BY GARSON KANIN

IN the middle of the gingerbread summer town of Oak Bluffs on the island of Martha's Vineyard, Massachusetts, stands a vast, spreading, ornate shed known as the Tabernacle. It has been in continuous use since July 1879, and is said to have sounded to the soaring exhortations of the Messrs. Moody and Sankey, the Reverend Billy Sunday, and Aimee Semple McPherson—as well as less celebrated but no less passionate voices. Circumscribing the meeting ground on which the Tabernacle stands, the rows of cottages seem to be holding hands in the spirit of the surround. Not one of these toy cathedrals was built in this century, and each appears to be attempting to outdo the others in the frills and fancies of "The American Carpenters' Renaissance." This sense of neighborly competition reaches a climax every year when, on the third Wednesday in August, the Grand Illumination is held. ("In the event of inclement weather the Grand Illumination will be held on the *fourth* Wednesday in August." That circumstance, let it be noted, has occurred only five times in the ninety-six years of the ceremony. Some of the sterner Methodists hint darkly at the reasons for these storms. Once, in 1904, a thunder shower descended on the fourth Wednesday, as well, and the Grand Illumination was not held at all. *Every* local Methodist knows the reason for *this* one.)

On the night of the Grand Illumination, the cottages are strung with candlelit Japanese lanterns, some as old as the cottages themselves. Hundreds of them are family treasures, brought to Massachusetts from the Orient by the seafaring men who once made this island their home. The meeting ground, too, is strung with lanterns, which, following the first part of a Band Concert and Community Sing, are lighted, one by one. By nightfall the area is aglow. An exact count is clearly impossible, but those who know say that between ten thousand and fifteen thousand candles are lighted on the night. Squads of volunteers of all ages swiftly replace those which burn out, or blow out, or go out, and the glittering effect is maintained until the band plays "The Star-Spangled Banner," usually about ten P.M.

The greater part of the island's population, both permanent (6,448) and summer (42,771), attends this event, which combines beauty, fantasy, tradition, devotion, magic, the real, the unreal, the past, present and future, mystery and faith.

This year, fog rolled over the island in the late afternoon and promised to bring a new dimension to the Grand Illumination. Veterans of the occasion discussed the matter in the shops and in the streets. There was general agreement that if the fog remained, the lights might be especially effective.

The fog represented something else again to Ethan Eliot, as he sat in the plane hovering above Martha's Vineyard. It represented terror. Although he had served as a paratrooper during the war with the 82nd Airborne Division, he was habitually unnerved in a plane. Once, during a flight to England through a North Atlantic storm, his wife, Rosemary, had said to him, "What I don't get is how anybody who hates it the way you could've been in the—what did they call them?—pariotroops?"

He replied an hour and a half later, while they waited for their luggage at London Airport.

"I'll tell you," he said, "I was always so *terrified* in the plane that I was overjoyed by the chance to jump out."

She regarded him as she inquired, "What are you talking about?"

"Didn't you just ask me something?"

"No."

"Oh."

This evening, looking out at the heavy fog, he found himself wishing for his chute and jump-boots. The airport at Martha's Vineyard was not, after all, JFK. The pilot had been circling for a time (Ethan had no idea how long, and could not bring himself to look at his watch), hoping for a break in the weather. Apparently he had found one, or a substitute, for the plane was losing altitude rapidly (too rapidly?) as it plunged forward. Ethan tried, unsuccessfully, to relax.

ETHAN ELLIOT,
SCENE DESIGNER,
IN MASS. CRASH

The headline, complete with his often misspelled name, appeared before him. He corrected it for his listing in *Time:*

DIED: *Brilliant, nonconformist theatrical designer Ethan Eliot, 39, in Martha's Vineyard air crash, bringing untimely close to a brief, spectacular Broadway career.*

The plane made a perfect, smooth landing while he was trying to fit the word "original" into the obituary. The plane taxied to the unloading area.

Ethan picked up his heavy briefcase, three rolls of blueprints, the unread weekend magazines, half a pound of caviar in dry ice (for Rosemary), and a bulky F.A.O. Schwarz package (for Belle, their four-year-old daughter). She had especially asked for "a doll, a boy doll." When Ethan pointed out she already owned seven dolls, she explained, "Yes, I love a family."

As he stepped off the plane, an oddly dressed, handsome young man approached him and saluted.

"The bloomin' car is wytin', sir," he said, with a brilliantly performed Cockney accent.

He wore the conventional island dress: sandals, shorts, and tee shirt—but, in addition, a chauffeur's old-fashioned cap, a leather bow tie around his neck, and leather puttees. (Where the hell did *they* come from?) He began to unencumber Ethan, officiously. The onlookers were amused by the act, but Ethan was disconcerted.

"All right, Alan, cut the comedy," he said, and hurried off to the car. It was not in its usual place, which further irritated him. Alan approached, having shed the cap, puttees, and tie.

"It's over there, Mr. Eliot," he said, pointing to the opposite side of the lot. "I got here a little late, I guess, and this was jammed up."

They walked to the car in silence.

Alan explained. "I called over, and when they said an hour late, I thought I might as well hang around and help at the house. Actually, you're an hour and thirty-five minutes late."

"I know."

They reached the car.

"Where's everybody?" asked Ethan.

As a rule, Rosemary brought Belle to meet his plane every Friday evening.

"I was about to tell you. They're having dinner—the schedule got all fouled, what with the late plane and all. So Rosie...Mrs. Eliot thought they ought to go ahead."

"What did you say?"

"So, *see*, Mrs. Eliot thought they ought to go ahead," Alan enunciated clearly.

"All right."

Alan put the briefcase and packages in the back, and took the driver's seat. Ethan got into the car, wearily.

They started off. It was 8:10 p.m., but a strong summer light still limned the fields, the sea and sky of this tranquil Eden he had known almost all his life.

Alan said, "Maybe you forgot, but tonight's the Grand Illumination."

"Yes," said Ethan, "I did forget."

"The singing and stuff, that's on *already*, but they don't go with the lantern bit till about nine."

Ethan looked at his watch, and checked it with the clock on the dashboard.

"Hell," he said.

"If we move as soon as we hit the house," said Alan, "we can make it there by maybe quarter to nine. So no sweat."

"I haven't had anything to eat," said Ethan, embarrassed at once by his petulant tone.

"She said something about a box lunch ready."

The idea of eating cold food out of paper, while standing about in a crowd, or worse, sitting on the damp grass, with thousands of people singing all around, appalled him.

"Also," Alan added, "they sell stuff over there tonight, you know. Hot coffee and sandwiches, and hot dogs, Dairy Whip."

The very sound of it made Ethan queasy.

"Never mind," he said.

What if he didn't go? Let *them* go. He would stay at home, and Sam could fix him a proper meal. He would be rested and ready by the time they returned. Of course. It was no more than sensible, and everyone would understand. It was not his fault the plane had been delayed. What if this were one of the weekends he hadn't been able to come at all? A matter of an hour or two. And as far as the Grand Illumination was concerned, he had seen it dozens of times.

As this solution occurred to him, the tension abated for the first time in hours. He took a deep breath of the ever-astonishing air. He looked at a field of ready corn, and could taste it. How quickly, he reflected, the island takes hold. All at once, he was struck by a concept for *On with the New,* one of the plays on which he was working. It involved a series of simple panels on pivots, eliminating the cumbersome turntable plan that had been troubling the director, Marc Antik. He had not been thinking about the show at all.

As his world fell into place, he turned to Alan, touched his shoulder, and said, "Sorry, kiddo."

"No sweat."

"And about being such a sourpuss about your dress-up gag, too."

"No, I guess it *would* have been, the way we first figured. If we'd all been there. This way, there was no audience."

"Yes there was."

"The wrong one." They laughed together. "Uta fixed up the cap and...Mrs. Eliot found these puttees at the What Not Shop when we stopped there one night. And the tie—well, that was my own."

"Very funny. But when we get really fatigued, the first thing we lose is our sense of humor. Have you ever noticed that?"

"To tell the truth, Mr. Eliot, I don't remember ever being what you call fatigued."

"You don't?"

"No, sir."

Ethan smiled. It was most agreeable, having these youngsters around. He felt pleased with himself for having organized the summer so well.

The house at East Chop had been built by his fauther, a Taunton, Massachusetts, architect, in 1926, and bequeathed, six years ago, to Ethan and his sister, Priscilla. They had agreed to use it alternately, summer by summer, the other renting nearby.

The fourth summer, they tried sharing it—with unhappy results. Priscilla and Rosemary were too different to mesh lives, even for a holiday time. Priscilla, who taught Modern English Poetry at Smith, was not ideally partnered with Rosemary, who at fifteen had lied about her age in order to make the Copa line. She had graduated to Broadway, where she did four stand-out bits in four musicals, before retiring (on her eighteenth birthday) to marry Ethan.

When the ill-advised experiment came to an end, Ethan offered his sister his share of the property, gratis.

Her response: "If I never see it again, pal, I'll feel blessed. You take it," she added, "but I want to be paid for my share. I'm not as generous as you are. And in the circumstances, I don't see why I should be."

She and her husband and their four children began to spend their summers in Colorado.

So it was that the previous year Ethan and Rosemary had taken full and sole possession of the house. With its grounds and gardens, beach and dock and Sailfish and views, it was an ideal summer place—except for the problem of staffing.

Servants had come and gone throughout July, making it a frazzled month. Rosemary was a demanding mistress, insisting upon a high standard of service. In August, in desperation, Ethan had engaged a couple through a New York agency, at a giddy fee. They lasted three weeks. Ten days before Labor Day, the house was closed, and the restive summer mercifully shortened.

In the early spring of this year, when planning for the months ahead began, Rosemary became tense with the recollection of last summer's failure.

"Let's rent the damn thing out," she suggested. "How much could we get. Rent it to your sister—I notice she took *our* money—or anybody. And let's go to Europe. Or Greece, like everybody."

"And Belle?"

"Wouldn't your sister take her for a few weeks?"

"Sure, but I don't want her to. Besides, I'll have a show in the shop, and one on the board, and maybe, please God, the musical may come through. Charlie says it looks pretty good for me."

"Well, I don't know. But I *do* know I don't want to see that insane parade clomping through for three months—eating and drinking and getting paid for it."

"Would you let me organize it?" he asked. "I mean, try?"

"It's all yours. I can't wait to see what you come up with."

He began with no idea whatever, but asked Priscilla to lunch, and went over the matter with her.

"If I were you," she advised, "I'd get college kids."

"Really?"

"That's what *we* did last year. It was a roaring success. We had two University of Colorado girls, and they were flawless."

Why not? he thought. Summer hotels everywhere were staffed with students. He remembered how often he had been impressed by the wholesome, good-natured efficiency with which they went about their duties.

Priscilla sent him a list of placement bureaus, and he attacked the matter systematically, through correspondence, phone calls, and interviews.

In mid-May, he engaged a German exchange student, Uta Muller, as governess. She was twenty, and an honor pre-med student, interested in pediatrics. Her only drawback was her beauty. Fortunately, she was somewhat overweight and wore glasses.

To drive the car, look after the jeep, tend the grounds, and make himself generally useful, he hired Alan Bolt, a first-year student at the American Academy of Dramatic Arts. This bright young man wanted a job and got it because, although primarily an actor, he was interested in all phases of the theater and admired Ethan's designs. Ethan thought he might be additionally valuable as an assistant on weekend work: tracing, building models, and planning light-plots. It was further reassuring to know that someone would be around to look after Rosemary and Belle at the beach.

The Lauries were a stroke of great good fortune. They were a young couple, graduate students at Oberlin College, and devoted to a single aim: their plan for a restaurant to be called the All-American Kitchen, which would feature regional dishes from every part of the United States. To this end, Sam Laurie had been studying cooking and baking for the past two years, while Ella Laurie specialized in nutrition and management. Sam was anxious to have a few months in New England, and through an ad in the *Saturday Review* the contact had been made.

The combined salaries of these four came to less than that of a single member of last year's abortive attempts.

"It looks pretty fair on paper," Rosemary admitted. "Let's hope it works. Personally, I doubt it."

She was proved wrong. With the addition of a part-time laundress, the establishment was perfectly ordered. Ella Laurie took quiet charge, instructions were put into writing, menus were planned, buying was done in advance, schedules made and adhered to.

The season was difficult only for Ethan, who had to settle for short weekends. The one stretch of time at the end of July to which he had so looked forward was marred by Rosemary's ten-day illness. She thought it might be neuralgia or a form of rheumatism, brought on by the damp climate; but the doctor told Ethan, privately, that it was more likely a result of stress. Whatever it was, it was painful and necessitated rest by day and sedation by night.

One weekend had been ruined by a mix-up about a set-model with which Alan was helping. Through a misunderstanding, he sent it, unfinished, by parcel post to New York on Friday. Since it had to be completed and delivered by Monday, there was no point in Ethan coming up. Alan offered to come down and help, but Ethan decided against upsetting the smooth routine.

In general, however, Ethan's plans had been a triumph, and tonight, sitting beside Alan, nearing the house, he felt satisfied and strong.

He ran over his immediate plan. Greetings. Everyone off to the Grand Illumination, with the exception of the Lauries and himself. A long bath. Dinner. A nap until they returned. Belle's present. Later, a supper of this caviar and—why not?—champagne with Rosemary. Alone.

Rosemary had made other plans and was waiting on the porch, looking her prettiest in a gay Lilly Pulitzer. Belle jumped into the car, found her package, and started to tear it open, while Ethan greeted his wife.

Uta began to scold her charge, but Rosemary said, "Oh, lay off her, Fraulein, it's a holiday."

"As you wish, Mrs. E."

Rosemary put a miniature picnic basket in Ethan's hands and said, "How's that for clever. Let's go, it's late."

"I thought maybe I wouldn't tonight, because—" he began.

"Oh, really!" said Rosemary. "We wouldn't have waited."

"Please, Daddy," wheedled Belle.

Was it that look from Uta that made him change his mind? he wondered. Or did he feel like going after all? Or was he drawn to the promise of magic, along with the thousands?

In any event, he found himself in the back of the car, between Rosemary and Belle, speeding toward Oak Bluffs.

Belle babbled away, happily, overcome by her boy doll.

Rosemary held her husband's right hand, tightly, as he ate a thick sandwich with his left.

On the front seat, Uta and Alan sat quietly, a wide space between them.

Alan stopped the car on Circuit Avenue, near a narrow passage to the meeting ground.

"Where'll I find you?" he asked.

"Back of the stand," Rosemary replied.

"Oh, yeah. I know. See y'."

Uta took Belle's hand, and moved with her into the crowd.

"Pay attention," she said. "Hold on always to one of us, and if you are lost ever, stand still and don't wander."

"I *never* wander," said Belle, gravely.

Rosemary and Ethan joined hands.

"You had enough to eat?" she asked.

"Plenty," he said.

"You can get coffee. They have stands tonight."

"No matter."

"You look like you can *use* some coffee."

"I do?"

"Tired. Or worn."

"The flight, I imagine. It was a *bitch*."

"*What* was a bitch?" asked Belle.

"Look at all these *lanterns!*" said Uta.

"You better rest tomorrow," said Rosemary to her husband.

"Speaking of look—you're mighty shadowy-under-the-eyes yourself."

"Don't be silly."

"You are."

"It's this idiot light."

Ethan laughed. "I'll get Alan to relight you."

"What?" she asked.

"He's the expert, isn't he?"

"What is all this?"

"Nothing, darling. Just a joke."

"I look perfectly all right. I've never looked better."

" 'Peak-ed' is the word they use up here," said Ethan.

"For *you*, not *me*."

They reached the Tabernacle, which by this time, was overflowing.

The platform held a brass band of thirty, dressed in white; a lady with a bun, at the piano; and, at the microphone, a man in red, leading the singing.

"Now!" he shouted, in the same tone he had used in the days before amplification. "All together!"

Thousands of voices were raised in uninhibited song:

"The man who has plenty of good pea-*nuts*
And giveth his neighbor none..."

Rosemary and Ethan smiled at each other, as they linked arms.

"He shan't have any of my pea-*nuts*
When his pea-*nuts* are gone..."

"I can't see," cried Belle.
Uta lifted her from the ground, and held her in her arms.

"When his pea-*nuts* are go-o-one,
When his pea-*nuts* are go-o-one,
He shan't have any of my pea-*nuts*,
When his pea-*nuts* are gone!"

The crowd applauded itself, warmly.
"Now!" shouted the leader, "with 'rich, red, ripe strawberries!' "
The throng raised a happy groan.
"And be sure you get it all in on the one beat, now. Go!"
The singing continued:

"The man who has plenty of richredripestrawberries,
And giveth his neighbor none..."

"Why don't *you* sing, Uta?" asked Belle.
"I don't know the song," said Uta.
"*Nobody* does," said Belle.
"They do."
"Try."
"I will. Later."

"He shan't have any of my richredripestrawberries,
When his richredripestrawberries are gone."

Ethan studied his wife. He wished that she would join in the singing.

He looked about. The community singers included members of the seersucker group from Edgartown, beards and babushkas from Chilmark, families from Vineyard Haven, artists from Menemsha, Gay Head yachtsmen—white and colored and Portuguese, happily joined in the nonsense song.

"When his richredripestrawberries are go-o-one,
When his richredripestrawberries are go-o-one."

Children abounded. Ethan noted how many of them were perched high on the shoulders of fathers and big brothers.

"He shan't have any of my richredripestrawberries,
When his richredripestrawberries are gone!"

Alan arrived.

"I'm fine," he said. "Found a swell spot in Shubert Alley."

Rosemary laughed. Uta looked at Alan, uncertainly. Ethan realized she still had language difficulties; and saw, too, that she was having trouble with the squirming child in her arms.

"Here," he said. "Give her to me."

"I'm all right, truly," Uta insisted.

"I'll take her," offered Alan. "She's pretty heavy."

Belle, excited and delighted to have become a sought-after prize, began a coy, bobbing dance.

"Stop it!" said Rosemary.

"Come here to me," said Ethan.

He took Belle from Uta and lifted her high, in an attempt to move her over his head and onto his shoulders. She was giggling, and kicking her feet in a gay frenzy.

"Careful!" warned Uta.

A sharp cry of pain from Ethan froze Belle. As he lost his balance, she slipped from his arms. Alan leaped forward and caught her. Ethan put his hand to his nose.

"What is it?" cried Rosemary.

"Nothing," said Ethan.

"Take her away," said Uta to Alan.

Alan lifted Belle to his shoulders, and moved off.

"Nosebleed," Uta said. "May I?"

She led Ethan to a space on the lawn near a tree, and had him sit against it, his head held back.

A small boy, preparing to light lanterns, came by.

"Boy!" Uta called to him. "You want to make half a dollar?"

"Sure."

"Get me a bag of ice cubes."

"No kiddin'?"

"Honest."

The boy ran off.

"Breathe through the mouth," said Uta.

Ethans nose was bleeding badly.

"Are you sure the child shouldn't see this?" asked Rosemary.

"That would not be my judgment, Mrs. E. Blood. It sometimes terrifies."

"It sure in hell terrifies *me*. Do you think Alan brought a drink?"

"He usually does," said Uta.

"I don't want a drink," Ethan said, sounding as though he had a bad cold.

"For me," said Rosemary, "not for you."

"Oh."

She went off to hunt for Alan.

Uta took some pocket Kleenex from her bag, and used it expertly to stanch the flow of blood.

The boy came running back with a hand towel full of ice cubes.

"They didn't have a bag," he explained. "Okay?"

"Give him a buck," said Ethan.

Uta did so.

"Hey, thanks," said the boy. "But I got to get the towel back."

Uta put the ice cubes on the grass, and gave the boy his towel. He ran off, yelling happily. Uta put several ice cubes into Ethan's handkerchief, and applied the compress to the back of his neck.

Rosemary returned.

"How's the patient?" she asked.

"Impatient," said Ethan.

The treatment was effective, and in a few minutes Ethan rose and said, "Thanks. You're a fine nurse, Uta. Now let's forget it."

"You're not *tizzy?*" she asked.

"What? Oh—*dizzy!* No."

They all laughed.

Rosemary said, "Come on, I'll get you some coffee."

"Would *you* like some?"

"No, thanks."

"Then, look," said Ethan. "They're starting on the lanterns. You stick with Belle. I'll get some and be right with you."

"All right."

"Where'll you be? Same place?"

"Just about."

"I would care for some," said Uta.

"Come on, then."

Ethan and Uta moved through the descending darkness, into the beginning wonderland. Most of the electric lights in the area were being extinguished as the soft glow of candlelit lanterns began to take over. Before long, the cottages themselves seemed to be built of lighted lanterns, and acres of joyous color burned in the haze. The fog was, indeed, lending a singular quality to the Grand Illumination this year.

They found a stand, and drank lukewarm, bitter coffee, watching the event.

"*Ausgesucht!*" she whispered.

"What?"

"Perfect. Beauty."

"Sounds nice."

"Can we go? I want to see Belle's face, and also—"

"Listen, for kids brought up on Disney—it's not much. Me—it still knocks me out—and I've been seeing it all my life."

"But can we go?"

They walked again through the field of lighted lanterns, variegated and decorative and exotic. There were thousands more hanging beyond, growing dimmer as they receded into the clouds of billowing mist. The great chorus could be heard in the distance, singing with increased abandon as the seasoned leader cued it into more spirited songs.

Ethan began to experience the unsettling sensation of seeing things as he had never before seen them. Familiar objects—an ice-cream cone, a straw hat, a corncob pipe—were strange and different. Uta, too, was revealed to him anew. He saw, beneath her holiday manner, that she was melancholy and frightened.

"How do you feel?" she asked.

"Lightheaded, sort of. Tizzy."

"I, too."

"Oh? I thought mine might be loss of blood or some such."

"No, no. You lost not so much as to—No. It is this—so comic light, and the air. And, too, how they swing to and fro, the lights. You have seen hypnotists? It is how they often do, with swinging lights."

"I don't mind. It's a kind of a jag without grog."

"Ach!" she said. "So many words I do not yet know. I am uncouraged."

As they approached the Tabernacle, a new song began:

"Some think
The world was made for fun and frolic,
And so do I!
And so do I!"

Searching for Rosemary, they came upon her from behind. She stood beside Alan, who held Belle straddled across his neck. All three were singing loudly. Two things struck Ethan at once: Rosemary's arm around Alan's waist, and Belle singing the words by synchronizing her lip movements to those about her.

"Some think
It well to be all melancholic,
To pine and sigh,
To pine and sigh."

He moved to Rosemary's side. She looked up, gaily, continued to sing, and put her free arm around *his* waist. He tried to join the singing, but found that he could not.

"But I,
I love to spend my time in singing
Some joyous song,
Some joyous song.
To set
The earth with music gaily ringing
Is far from wrong,
Is far from wrong!"

Alan smiled at Ethan, and made a gesture urging him to sing. Now Rosemary and Alan, laughing, sang directly at each other.

"Listen! Listen!
Echoes sound afar."

Ethan peered about for Uta, until he saw her, half-hidden in shadow.

"Listen, listen,
Echoes sound afar."

Rosemary and Alan were swaying together to the music. Belle, on her perch, had stopped singing and begun screeching in happy, rollercoaster alarm.

"Funiculi, funicula,
Funiculi, funicula,
Joy is everywhere,
Funiculi, funicula!"

Uta stepped in and took Belle from Alan. She held the child on her shoulders all through "Juanita" and "Ta Ra Ra Boom Dee Ay." A round began:

"Hear the bells
So sweetly ringing,
Sweetly ringing."

Ethan said, "Shouldn't we swing around and see the lanterns?"
"Why not?" said Rosemary, in her party tone.

> "In the steeple,
> Gaily singing,
> Gaily singing."

"Let's see," said Ethan. "This way, I think. It's best to follow the stream."
He led the group to the outer path, the sound of the singers fading behind them.

> "Ding, dong,
> Ding, dong,
> Ding!"

They joined the parade moving slowly about the circle, studying the lanterns and the effects, cottage by cottage.
Uta tried letting Belle walk, but in the jostling crush it became foolhardy. Ethan picked her up and carried her.
"If you're going to kick me in the nose again," he said, "kick my other nose. You've already broken one."
"It's a *joke!*" Belle shouted. "Isn't it, Uta? Isn't it? I guessed it, because people only have *one* of nose."
The party laughed, and Belle's remark went into the family album.
Ethan watched Uta walking ahead beside Alan. Alan took her arm. Ethan glanced at his wife as she lit a cigarette quickly. Uta moved away, breaking Alan's hold. He stepped toward her and took her arm again.
"May I please have an ice-cream cone, please? Chocolate? asked Belle.
Rosemary exploded. "No! Now you be *quiet* for five minutes! You've been a nuisance all *day.*"
"Rosie!" said Ethan, shocked by her outburst.
"How would *you* know? Have you been around?"
"All right," he said. "Calm down."
He lagged behind to buy Belle an ice-cream cone. Uta appeared

and, once again, made use of her Kleenex. She bibbed Belle's dress, and gave her a Kleenex to use as a napkin.

The circular stroll went on, with Rosemary and Alan a few paces ahead of the crowd, Ethan, Uta and Belle behind. The mist had begun to rise. Feet were on solid ground, bodies and heads still enfogged, adding to the fantasy.

Uta asked, "Not everywhere—only here, the custom?"

"That's all," said Ethan. "There are all sorts of notions about what started it—and when." He continued, automatically, as his new eyes held Rosemary and Alan in focus. "My grandmother used to explain that *way* back there was an annual religious camp meeting held here, and on the last night the campers would burn all their leftover candles." He saw Alan glance back without seeing him. He saw Rosemary and Alan join hands. His sight zoomed in, filling his screen of vision with those hands in sensual communication. He heard his own voice, an inappropriate soundtrack. "Some of the old people on the porches were born in these cottages. Do you see how they all give parties tonight? And dress up? And the kids? Everyone has company. They come to look at us and we come to look at them. And their lanterns." Rosemary turned toward him. He looked down and away. Too late. Apparently she had located him. The hands unjoined. Time. A minute? Ten? "They say that even before there were cottages—or the Tabernacle—the meeting ground was famous. Daniel Webster spoke here. You never heard of him, so why do I tell you?" As he spoke, he saw Alan lean to Rosemary and whisper something. Her response was a laugh, followed by a playful slap on his buttocks, as though he were a mischievous child. He spanked her in return—the child strikes back. "There's another theory I've heard—that the Grand Illumination was thought up for the time when President Grant came here at the end of August in eighteen seventy-four. And it was such a smash that they kept doing it. I must say, that's the one seems sensible to me." Rosemary was clinging to Alan's upper arm with both her hands. As the crowd pressed in, his hands went to her body, ostensibly protecting her from the crush. Ethan had stopped talking. He looked about, bewildered, and found Uta observing him. He felt his skin go warm and moist as he realized she had seen what he had seen. He took her arm and hurried her along, catching up with Rosemary and Alan.

"Had enough?" he asked.

"I'll say!" replied Rosemary.

Belle leaned down and spoke softly into her father's ear. "Not yet."

"Better," he said.

"Did you see that big old one?" asked Alan. "Sort of torn? They say it's over a hundred years old. From Japan."

They made their way to the car.

Belle asked, "May I sit up front, please?"

"No," said Rosemary.

Belle sulked, then slept.

Rosemary held onto Ethan's upper arm with both her hands.

This time, Uta sat close to Alan.

Cool, sea-scented air blew through the car. Ethan felt his head clearing. As he returned to normalcy, he reproached himself. A jag, surely. He had probably misinterpreted everything in that bizarre atmosphere.

Halfway home, Alan and Uta exchanged a glance. Alan smiled. Rosemary let go Ethan's arm and lit a cigarette. She leaned back, closed her eyes, and breathed deeply.

"You all right?" asked Ethan.

"Headache," she replied.

"All right, now. None of that," he said firmly.

They exchanged a firm, searching look, poised dangerously on the launching pad of hostility.

In the front seat, Alan bent over the wheel in an effort to suppress his snickering.

"What's so funny?" asked Rosemary.

He straightened up. "Those old lanterns," he said. "Weren't they a riot?"

Uta inched away from him.

When they reached home, Uta took Belle up to bed, and Alan said good night, retiring to his room over the garage.

Ethan, in an effort to salvage the scratchy evening, resolved to carry out at least the final part of his original plan. He went down to the wine cellar to get a bottle of champagne out of the cooler. On his way back up, he heard a crunching noise on the gravel path. Through the windows of the dark kitchen, he saw Alan poised on a bicycle, making incomprehensible signs in the direction of the second story and mouthing a sentence before riding off toward town. Ethan turned on the light.

Still puzzling out the sight, he prepared toast for the caviar, and placed it on a tray. (Rosemary?) Carrying it, and the champagne, he went up. (Uta?) In the upstairs sitting room he set the table, and moved into the bedroom.

"All ready, love," he called into Rosemary's dressing room.

"In a minute, darling," she said.

He opened the bottle of champagne, poured out a taste, sat down, and sampled it. Perfect. He filled the glass, downed it, and felt better at once.

A scream and crash jolted him to his feet. He rushed into Rosemary's dressing room, found it empty, and proceeded to her bathroom. She was lying, face down and naked, on the floor. Her right leg was bent grotesquely.

"Rosie! What is it?"

"Oh, God," she moaned. She tried to rise and cried out again. He knelt beside her. "My back," she said. "My back!"

"What happened?"

"I slipped getting out. Oh, God, I can't move."

"I'll get Uta."

"No!" she yelled. "Keep that *Kraut* away from me!"

From the other room, an anxious voice called, "Mr. Eliot?"

Ethan went out. The Lauries had come down. Uta, too, stood quietly in the bedroom. She and Ethan stared at each other.

"She slipped and fell," said Ethan. "Call Dr. Hoxsie."

"Right," said Sam, and went off.

"If it's a sprain or so," said Uta, "There is Mr. Clements. Excellent. The physiotherapist.

"Fine," said Ethan. "Get him, too."

"If you need him," said Uta.

"Yes."

She left.

"Anything?" asked Ella.

"Stick around," Ethan answered.

He went back into the bathroom, carrying a blanket and a pillow. Rosemary was in tears.

"Doctor on the way," he said. "Meantime, I suppose better not to move, huh?"

"Give me a Seconal," she said.

"Shouldn't we wait and—"

"I'm in pain, damn it, don't you *believe* me?"

"Of course."

"Well, hurry up. I'll take two.

He bent down and gave her the pills.

By the time Mr. Clements arrived, she was asleep. He examined her and said she could be moved to her bed. He and Ethan picked her up, carefully, and carried her to it.

The doctor came in, and was relieved to find Mr. Clements.

"I'd have asked you to send for this bloke," he said. "It's more in his line, anyway, these wrenches. How bad is it?"

"I don't know as yet," said Mr. Clements.

He awakened Rosemary in order that he and the doctor could make an examination.

Mr. Clements began testing.

He asked, "Does this hurt?"

"Yes," she said.

"This?"

"Yes!"

"What about this?"

"Yes!"

He took his hands away from her body and asked, This?"

"Ow!" she moaned, as if in severe pain.

Mr. Clements looked at the doctor, solemnly.

Ethan felt faint.

"Thank you for coming, Mr. Clements," he said. "And you, Doctor."

He went out to the sitting room, and sent the Lauries back to bed. Uta returned to her room.

Alone, Ethan sat and slowly consumed the caviar and champagne. When there was no more of either left, he went to his dressing room and undressed. He put on fresh clothes, continued to his workroom, found a piece of writing paper and an envelope, stood at his drawing board, and wrote:

4:30 A.M.
the morning after
The Grand Illumination

Dear Rosie, Dear Alan,

The jig is up, and the chips are down.

I commend you to each other's tender care.

You are getting a fine girl, Alan. She has a few faults, but who has none? The more you can manage to let her have her way, the better your chances of succeeding where I failed. Good luck.

Rosemary, my wife, I loved you as long and as much as you let me. For the good we created, my thanks. For the blunders, my apologies.

But, oh, this last sham of yours tonight was degrading for us both. A little more and we would have become completed demoralized.

So how much better to end now, while we are at least partly civilized. Good luck to you, too.

Many gnawing mysteries are clear to me tonight—this morning. Your unfortunate ten-day "illness" in July. Sorry to have been responsible for putting you through that strained performance.

And Alan—sending the model down "by mistake" that Friday. Clever. You transfer that sort of imagination to your work, and you'll go far.

As God is my judge, Rosie, in spite of everything I was gratified to learn you did not *really* fall and injure yourself tonight.

By the way, Alan, it's all right to call her "Rosie" now. Rosie...Mrs. Eliot. So see Mrs. Eliot. Cute.

In the clear light of dawn, champagne, reason, and, of course, the Grand Illumination—I see that this new mode is better and healthier for all concerned. The truth is so simple and plain that it is often hard to see. Garish matters catching attention more easily. The world is a coloring book and we all have our own ideas, don't we? about what looks the prettiest. That phrase: "the unvarnished truth." As Saroyan once wrote in *Jim Dandy*—a marvelous play of his I did years ago at Ogunquit—"He knew the truth and was looking for something better." That's me. Why is it I feel—above all else—relieved?

Rosie. The only serious problem is Belle. For the moment, the way I propose to solve it is to take her with me. I am not sure where as yet, but will let you know.

Bill F. will be in touch with regard to legal matters, and I'll tell Mrs. Urbont at the studio to handle house troubles and bills and bookkeeping—(that looks quaint with two k's, but I'll stand by it. I feel *everything* is right tonight).

Remember, the summer is ending, not ended.

Sleep well, both.

Faithfully (Ha!) yours,
Ethan Eliot

He addressed the envelope:

Mrs. Ethan Eliot
Mr. Alan Bolt
Personal

and put it into his pocket. He went down the hall to Belle's room. The door connecting it to Uta's room was open. Uta was sitting up in bed, reading. When Ethan stopped into the doorway, she did not seem surprised to see him.

"We're leaving," he said. "Belle and I."

"Yes," she said calmly, and got out of bed.

The choice details of her generous body could be glimpsed through the folds of her transparent nightgown. Ethan missed the charge such a moment normally brought. The sight seemed, in fact, uninteresting, even tiresome. He hoped, ruefully, that his disaffection would not be permanent.

As Uta put on her robe and slippers, Ethan said, "Would you pack what she'll need for ten days or so? Everything else of hers can be sent to the studio later on. I'll arrange about my own."

"Yes."

Uta set to work. Ethan went to the side of Belle's bed and touched her, tenderly.

"Hey!" she said, as she turned onto her back. She smiled. "Is it morning?"

"Sort of. We're going on a surprise trip."

"We are?"

"Yes. Just the two of us."

"Is it a secret?" she whispered.

"All right," he said, lowering his voice. "Yes."

"I'll have to bring the new doll, because he isn't named yet."

"By all means."

While she was dressing, Ethan and Uta said goodbye.

"I can come with you," she said.

"I think not."

"Later, *maybe?*"

"No."

"But I must leave here. Tomorrow."

"I would. Take a holiday—with pay, of course—before you go back to school."

"Thank you."

"We'll be in touch."

"Yes," she said. "The two losers."

"Uta," he said, "you never know about such things."

"They embraced in sudden tears.

From the ferry station at Vineyard Haven, Ethan phoned the Ritz-Carlton in Boston and reserved a two-bedroom suite:

By the time the early ferry had crossed the body of water which separates Martha's Vineyard from the mainland, Belle was asleep again. Ethan bedded her down on the back seat and drove steadily, each mile of the two-hour drive thinning the tie, until it was a gossamer thread, until it was nothing.

At the Ritz-Carlton he ordered a sumptuous party breakfast sent to the suite.

Later, washing up, it struck him, sickeningly, that he had forgotten to leave the letter he had so carefully composed. He leaned over the basin in despair.

"Oh, for God's sake!" he said.

He went out to the bedroom and found the letter, still in his pocket. He considered mailing it, having it delivered by messenger, wiring its contents. Instead, he decided to reread it. Having done so, he took it into the bathroom, tore it to bits, and flushed it down the drain.

He joined Belle at the breakfast table, where she was already eating heartily and feeding her doll.

"Well!" he said.

They recited, in unison, a family table joke. "The way *one* pig *waits* for *another!*"

"Are we going to stay here long?" she asked. "It's super!"

"A few days."

"What will we do all the time?"

"Entertain each other."

"How?"

"I'll show you."

"Then will we go home?"

He leaned forward, reached out, and grasped her wrist. "Listen, Belle. Love. We're going to start a new game. Right now."

"How do you play it?"

"Like this. Wherever we are—from this morning on—is home."

She thought for a long moment before she said, "That's a very good game."

"And pretty soon, in New York, we'll be in a new place. You and I."

"What about Mummy?" she asked with her mouth full of codfish cake.

"She'll be in the old place. I think that's what she wants."

"Will she come and see us?"

"Of course."

"Will Uta?"

"No."

"Will Alan?"

"Yes."

"Oh, good. I love Alan. Do you?"

"I like him."

"Mummy *loves* him," she said, her face buried in the cocoa cup.

"I know."

"And Uta loves him."
"Yes. You've got a chocolate moustache."
"Uta loves *me*, too." She wiped her upper lip. "Do you?"
"Yes. And I *like* you too."
"Oh?" she asked. "Like *and* love?"
"Yes yes. Both both."
"You're a silly man," she said.
"No, I'm not."

Garson Kanin has a long list of credits as actor, director and writer. He appeared on the Broadway stage in Boy Meets Girl, Three Men on a Horse *and other plays. He wrote and directed* Born Yesterday *for which he received the Sidney Howard Memorial Award and the Donaldson Award. He has written and directed a host of plays and movies. Some films were co-authored with his actress wife, the acclaimed Ruth Gordon. His writings have also appeared in prestigious publications. Mr. Kanin is active in the Authors League and other professional organizations.*

"We'll make this decision the way that we always do."

All the Way

BY PENELOPE GARLICK

THE beautiful wedding present carriage clock struck half past three on a dull afternoon in October. Unfailingly punctual, it marked the half hours by a nearly inaudible "cluck"—the sound made by a hen settling down on its nest—but the hour was achieved with a whir and a paean of triumph that seemed everlasting.

Mrs. Raglan was always alert to the "cluck" which brought an oasis, their tea time, within half an hour's crawl through her desert of long afternoons. The siesta enjoyed by her husband, stretched out, or nowadays sagging, head dropping on chest in his leather armchair, was not for herself an acquirable habit. In the window seat corner chosen, in daytime, for its view of the garden, she sat very upright, her only concessions to eighty-two years a stool for her feet and an old fashioned hassock begged from the Vicar for the small of her back. Here she knit meaningless time into plain stitch or purl and dropped both in over-ambitious, self-engineered stints which, if seldom successful, at least kept her mind on the knitting instructions and off the fast burgeoning plan that she started to find so attractive. Lately however this plan had become too insistent, too tempting a thing to be folded away with her knitting at tea time. It would very soon have to be voiced, to be shared, to be tactfully "gift wrapped" for Hughie's inspection.

Antoinette Raglan attentively counted her purls and forgot them immediately, turning her ancient, still beautiful face to the leaf bestrewn lawn. Here was a face whose exceptional structure, in age as in youth, could well have been penciled by Greuze or dreamed by Rossetti; indeed her whole frame was a triumph of mind over matter, even her eyes, once enormous, now merely triangular chippings of blue in a fragile mosaic, had kept their bright color, refusing to darken unless with the pain that she hid from her husband.

She fastened them now on the dusk which was leaching the last of the light from the Michaelmas daisies. Her plan, she was thinking, was growing too big for the room where she sat. Now it had surged, taking wing like the plovers who wheeled all day long between moorland and sea. It had taken her over, was taking possession especially at times such as now when the pain that she tried to keep secret was on the attack with a stab like a furious wasp at her breast.

Across the room, Hughie was snoring. Her hand, stealing under her jersey and finding the place of the wasp was cajoling it—"There, there, that's enough"—as she would an implacable child. The place of the wasp was on fire but her hand was like ice. With Hughie it was always his feet which were frozen in spite of his new sheepskin slippers and two pairs of socks. Neither had felt really comfortably warm since the summer. The new oil-fired heating that Gerry, most thoughtful of sons, had arranged for them, hadn't improved things at all. He simply had failed to believe that this coldness of theirs had little to do with the air but was creeping like frost in their blood. The thermostat heating performed like a dream of course, switching itself on and off with a businesslike click as if to dear Gerry's command all the way from his H.Q. in Ireland where he was giving real orders to people far better adjusted to change than his parents.

The last of his visits on leave had been linked with her poor unavailing attempt to preserve their log fire. She had used all her wits to convince him: "But darling, those pine logs aren't really too heavy to haul on the days Mrs. Benny can't come. You see, when she had her third baby last year, we discovered a new way to carry them. The old badminton net and a box make a sleigh which we pull from the shed to the kitchen and then—"

"But mother—"

"I believe the ancient Egyptians used sleighs for building the Pyramids—"

"Mother—"

"And so did the Easter Islanders placing those statues—"

"Mother, I simply can't bear to think of you dragging those—"

"Don't fuss so much darling. Your father and I aren't ungrateful, really we're not. It's just that we do like to look at a fire, a proper log fire. There are pictures to see in it, things that remind us..."

He had hugged her. Gerry would usually listen to reason but this time the battle was lost before it had started. And Hughie—she remembered how cross she had been with him afterwards—hadn't helped her at all. She couldn't think why. He adored a wood fire more than anything, toasted those feet of his...

Five minutes to tea time. Thursday, the day to make anchovy toast. And when she was ready to bring it, Hughie, who worked to some inner routine like the heating, would sense she was coming and open his eyes and still half-asleep would bark crossly—"What's that?" as if she'd mishandled a sword on parade.

...Wasp, wasp, leave me in peace while I'm boiling the kettle and spreading the anchovy...

"What's that?" Having delivered his bark General Raglan peered at the clock, settling back with a long exhalation of breath. "Tea, Nettie? Good. Only an hour and a half till the News."

She smiled. The News was important to Hughie. Important whatever it said—which was always the same only worse. What he really enjoyed was a glorious bellyache when it was over. Sometimes, she didn't always know why, the News would amuse him and then he would roar "Tommy Rot" and bellow with laughter. How splendid he was when he laughed; it came curling up fast from his chest to his throat and out—smack—like the break of a wave. If only it wasn't so painful to do it...afterwards...when the laughing had stopped and the choking began...

She had filled her own cup and now sitting as close to him as she could manage since Hughie's right ear was converting to stone like his feet, she wheedled him: "Don't let's play 'Scrabble' tonight. Let's have fun. Let's play 'Truths' instead, darling."

What surprise on his part and what thorough review of this odd deviation from custom; extracting the essence, chewing the meaning, a dog with a marrow bone!

How suspicious and careful he is, his wife thought, and, astounded at finding herself for the very first time in their long married life the more forceful and bold, knew that the plan she was paving the way for tonight was assured.

" 'Truths,' Nettie? That's that old houseparty game."

"I know. Please do Hughie, I'm serious."

She was too by God. Well, there was nearly an hour to the News. As for the game, at eighty-two surely there isn't much left to discover.

"Or could I be eighty-three?" he demanded.

"Eighty-four. I shall ask the first question." She leaned to his better ear. "Hughie—the truth now. Were you unfaithful to me with that little tart Dorothy Craven?"

"Dorothy Craven?...Ah! Pretty black haired bitch...Summer or '28. Aldershot."

"Well?"

"All right, Nettie. I *was*. Didn't mean anything."

"I should hope not. She had two quite revolting brown moles on her chin. I can see them now."

"So can I—but not the ones *you* mean."

The start of a laugh like a far distant rumble of thunder, then the violent explosion, the choking. "Nettie...take...my cup...I shall...drop it.

"There, darling. And don't be so silly and coarse. Play properly. Now it's your turn."

"Don't rush me. Don't rush me. Give me some more of that toast."

A long pause full of thought, masticating, reflective.

Then—"Nettie, were *you unfaithful to me with that bounder Tom*

Broome?"

"Yes. Once."

"Mm...But why for God's sake? And why only once?"

"Why was because of that fool Dotty Graven and you. Where was a punt in the boathouse during the Doubleday's Ball. Only once was because he showed me a cutting that told how he'd won the M.C."

"And that—"

"Shocked me darling. Showing me, not getting it, naturally."

"Typical of a bounder like him."

"Getting it, Hughie, was typical too."

"Don't try to make me jealous at eighty-two, Nettie. You never knew much about men."

"Eighty-four. Don't munch your teeth Hughie. And now it's my turn. I'll fill your cup first."

Spoon and cup danced a jig in their saucer in passage between the thin ivory hand and the larged mottled brown one.

"This is 'Truths' remember, so there's no getting out of it, Hughie. And it's something I've always wanted to know. *Your* decoration, your V.C. my darling. Was it earned in plain courage or anger—or how?"

No pause for reflection; he had given himself the answer too often.

"I suppose the action that won it was both, but in fact I was more than a little drunk at the time."

And his laugh with its gasping curtailment was painful to both, as was also poor truth, bare as the plate that had once held the anchovy toast.

Quickly she murmured—"I love you for telling me that. It took courage."

He smiled at her, leaning to lower the burner under the tea kettle, licked by too high a flame, presently saying:

"You put too much spirit you know."

"*You* put the new wick in too high."

"Can't see it properly nowadays. Waste of time anyhow."

She was suddenly angry. "Don't you see that if little things like the hot water for filling the tea pot, and drawing the curtains with NO GAPS—something you do so slapdashly on *your* day—aren't done, then our standards are slipping and then we'll be past it...past everything."

It was a tumble of words, stopping short with a cruel little catch of her breath. Wasp, Oh please wasp—her hand sliding under her cardigan. And for once, in an immediate respite, unexpected relief.

Did pain make one ugly? "Hughie, you say you can't see the wick properly nowaways, can you see *me?* What do I look like *now,* at this moment?"

"Is this still 'Truths'?"

"Yes." She waited impatiently while he chose words.

"I'm afraid you're rather a blur to me now. On a bad day you're just a pale little silhouette drifting about. I have to look very hard even with spectacles. What do I look like to you, Nettie?"

"Well I see you all right. Heavy and gray like a rock at Stonehenge. But it's not the *real* you. That's the one in my mind."

Yes, he knew very well what she meant, he thought, watching her pick up the tray and depart. The real Nettie wasn't here either, doing that knitting, fussing about those damned curtains, hiding that pain in her breast (or thinking she was)...She was really still Antoinette Raglan, so lovely a woman that people would stop in the street to stare after her...She was dressed in black, always in black at the regiment's ball, to show off her diamonds...or shoulders...or arms...Nettie's arms...and those eyes a brave blue for a man to be drowned in.

But those were her looks. She had everything else...gentleness, courage, recklessness too...and a wildness in bed...

Nettie, Nettie, we've known it all, haven't we? Remember the night we made Gerry? Grand National night. One needn't be sober to ride the Grand National but by God one's got to be sober to win it...

"All the way"—that's the old racing expression. I had it inscribed in your wedding ring, knowing we'd make it...

I'm a swine but I've always adored you, you know, General Raglan informed the armchair by his side and hearing a crash and a furious "damn" from the kitchen, called—"Why are you throwing the china about?" just to be tiresome.

The clock was making it's comfortable "cluck" on Mrs. Raglan's return from the kitchen. "Half an hour to the News," said her husband.

"Good." She sat down. "Then we've plenty of time to make our decision. You see Hughie darling, it's time to be practical. I was thinking just now, washing up, that practical is the right thing to *be*. Then I broke a damn saucer."

"What decision?"

"To die at the same time—this evening perhaps. Well, why not this evening and get it all over? By our own hands. How pompous that sounds. But of course it would just be by sleeping pills wouldn't it? I've been saving them up for a long time you know. At our ages it's easy to make it so no one...so Gerry...wouldn't know that we meant to."

The room was quite warm but she shivered a little settling again in her chair to the side of the needlework screen behind which were some of the wonderful logs that would never be lit, she told herself sadly. Stealing a glance at her husband she threw out a feeler—"The only alternative is to be patient and wait to be more ill and...separate."

There, the whole plan had come out for discussion at last.

The old man had removed his warm slippers, bending to massage his feet, rubbing each toe in its turn until, feeling some life in them, he could sit back, puffing a little but showing no trace of surprise at her words. His comment came now as a question—

"Nettie, where would you live without *me?* It's not grief that kills people you know, nor is it loneliness, it's the thought of being a burden to others."

"I know."

"Would you live on your own?"

"I'm not capable of it. I'd always be leaving the iron or the stove on. I can't change a fuse and I simply don't want to."

"Be serious, girl. Would you live with Gerry and Sue?"

"No, above all, NO. Never to be a bore or a duty unless it's to you."

"So you've never thought what you might do without *me?*"

"It's not a thinkable thought. Have you thought what *you'd* do the other way round?"

"Yes."

"Could you go on without me?"

"No."

The single word danced in her mind, lit a fire in her heart. "Then I'll get a pencil and paper," she told him. "We'll make this decision the way that we always do."

General Raglan was smiling. Some years ago saddling a horse at one end of the stables, he had overheard Gerry at sixteen informing a school friend: "As an army family we've got a habit of making our really important decisions by a military method that always comes up with the answer. It's a sort of Appreciation of Situations. So, in making this choice of a second-hand car or a horse or a motorbike..."

With Nettie and him, the old Staff College principle, used as a honeymoon joke had followed them into the years as a family tradition far more respected by her and his son than by him.

She had pushed her chair closer to his and took up her pencil, insisting: "Dictate the headings please darling. I always forget the order they come in."

"Write: 1. OBJECTIVE," he told her.

She wrote, adding under it—"Our deaths"—in her open impetuous hand.

"Then: 2. CONSIDERATIONS PERTAINING TO THE ATTAINMENT OF."

"I've got that. Go on."

"3. COURSES OPEN TO US. ADVANTAGES THEREFROM."

"Mm."

"4. COURSES OPEN TO THE ENEMY. DISADVANTAGES THEREFROM. And 5. CONCLUSION."

She wrote and looked up. "Hughie, who *is* the enemy?"

The question dropped into a silence so charged for them both that the click of the thermostat reaching the maximum heat decreed for their comfort by Gerry, seemed like an intrusion.

"Oh but I know, I know," she whispered, answering herself. "It's *life* that's the enemy. To all old people like us life is the final indignity."

His hand groped for hers and then covered it, letting her reasoning run to the end. When in her triumph, she cried to him—"*That's* the CONCLUSION!" her voice, to his ears, had recaptured the vigor of youth.

The clock started to whir before striking the hour.

"Time for the News," the old man said gently. "And after it's finished I'll light you a fire."

"They looked very peaceful," the doctor informed Gerald Raglan before the joint funeral. "Mrs. Benny called me as soon as she found them the day before yesterday morning. Your parents were failing quite rapidly lately you know."

"Yes, I know. Where where they—?"

"They died in their sleep. That's not an unusual occurrence with people their age, Colonel Raglan. They were sitting in front of the fire hand in hand. There were still some logs smoldering, she said."

"A fire? But—"

The heating was fully switched on but that evening was colder than usual. "The doctor's voice carried a hint of impatience. "You'll forgive me for not staying? I've several more visits to make before dark."

Penelope Garlick lives in Zimbabwe where she enjoys writing, gardening and graphology. She was born in England, educated there and in France and Switzerland. She is a direct descendant of Richard Brimsley Sheridan, the 18th century playwright. Penelope Garlick's story "Skaters Waltz" was in SSI No. 33.

Coming up in future issues of SSI

USA	**Irwin Shaw** Mixed Doubles
Mexico	**Carlos Fuentes** A Pure Soul
Philippines	**F. Sionil José** Tong
Turkey	**Aziz Nesin** The Rusty Tin Can in the Treasury
England	**E.G Peacock** The Chief Clerk
New Zealand	**Vincent O'Sullivan** The Witness Man
Malaysia	**Alias Ali** The Changing Tide
Gibraltar	**E.G. Chipulina** Case History
China (PRC)	**Li Guangtian** A Sunless Morning
Belgium	**Albert Russo** The Age of the Pearl
South Africa	**Jane Meiring** Rendezvous
Ireland	**T.G. Nestor** The Standing Stone
Israel	**Aharon Megged** The Name
Egypt	**Yehia Hakki** An Empty Bed
Australia	**Ian Nash** A Promise to Settle
USA	**Tillie Olsen** I Stand Here Ironing

And, for your reading pleasure, other intriguing, insightful stories from all lands.

Gift for:
Name ___
Address ___
City ___ State ___ Zip ___
Country ___
Please check □ New Subscription □ Renewal

Gift for:
Name ___
Address ___
City ___ State ___ Zip ___
Country ___
Please check □ New Subscription □ Renewal

Gift for:
Name ___
Address ___
City ___ State ___ Zip ___
Country ___
Please check □ New Subscription □ Renewal

Gift for:
Name ___
Address ___
City ___ State ___ Zip ___
Country ___
Please check □ New Subscription □ Renewal

Gift for:
Name ___
Address ___
City ___ State ___ Zip ___
Country ___
Please check □ New Subscription □ Renewal

Gift for:
Name ___
Address ___
City ___ State ___ Zip ___
Country ___
Please check □ New Subscription □ Renewal